STEAL AWAY

Also by Garry Disher
APPROACHES (short stories)
WRITING FICTION: AN INTRODUCTION TO THE CRAFT
THE PENGUIN ANTHOLOGY OF COMMUNITY WRITING (ed.)

STEAL AWAY
GARRY DISHER

All characters in this book are
entirely fictitious, and no reference
is intended to any living person.

Creative writing programme assisted by
the Literature Board of the Australia Council,
the Federal Government's arts funding and
advisory body.

ANGUS & ROBERTSON PUBLISHERS

Unit 4, Eden Park, 31 Waterloo Road,
North Ryde, NSW, Australia 2113, and
16 Golden Square, London W1R 4BN,
United Kingdom

This book is copyright.
Apart from any fair dealing for the
purposes of private study, research,
criticism or review, as permitted
under the Copyright Act, no part may
be reproduced by any process without
written permission. Inquiries should
be addressed to the publishers.

First published in Australia
by Angus & Robertson Publishers in 1987
First published in the United Kingdom
by Angus & Robertson UK in 1987

Copyright © Garry Disher 1987

National Library of Australia
Cataloguing-in-publication data.

Disher, Garry, 1949–
  Steal away.
  ISBN 0 207 15463 5.
  I. Title.
A823'.3

Typeset by Setrite Typesetters Ltd.
Printed in Beijing

ACKNOWLEDGEMENTS

The author wishes to acknowledge the assistance of a grant from the Literature Board of the Australia Council in the writing of this novel.

Creative writing programme assisted by the Literature Board of the Australia Council, the Federal Government's arts funding and advisory body.

1
GOOD AUDIENCE

When Robert Saxby was eight years old he realised that his father was often fearful and anxious. His father was a man who hated to find himself alone, a man who bloomed only when he had made himself snug with people and pets and bustle. Then Mr Saxby might uncoil. He liked to gesture, his hands grainy with printer's ink from his workshop, and would grow sentimental and expansive, calling people by the wrong names, shaking his head and clicking his tongue, pumping visitors and new acquaintances for more. "And what happened then?" he would ask. His face moved in delight, concern, triumph and a kind of knee-thumping glee as he listened to the answers. He leaned forward for more. Robert saw that people liked his father — he was a good audience.

Many of the visitors to the Saxby house in those years after the war were Mr Saxby's mates from his army days. Robert, a boy in short pants and with hair that wouldn't stay down at the back, sat on a wooden chair in the kitchen and listened to them yarn. He absorbed their voices, he imagined himself wearing berets like the ones that they had tucked into their pockets before they entered the house, and he watched the way they rolled their cigarettes with one hand and held the burning tip turned inwards to their palms.

And, when the visitors went home, or stayed on but had nothing more to offer, Robert's father had things of his own to say, uttering calumnies with such certainty that the family continued with its roast potato, knitting or crayons and said a short "Mm", avoiding his eyes and the self-doubt that they sensed was there, hoping that a guest might take up the point and help him weave his way through it. Finally somebody would say something and Mr Saxby would say a quick "You could be right," and blow his nose like a trumpet.

2
Impatient with Austerity

Robert's father liked to say that he'd be a much happier man if his ship came in. But money was tight in those years after the war, and he kept getting knocked back at the bank. He was a printer of wedding invitations, grocers' flyers, newsletters for the Labor Party and whatever else, and, if he could only buy a better press and rent a bigger building, why, he could expand.

"Well," he said one day. "It can't hurt to have another try, can it. Come on, kids, into the car." He wore a tweed suit and a little feather in the brim of his broad-brimmed hat. Robert's mother was smartly dressed in a suit, and her fingers kept her bosom free of ash from her cigarette, but a spring in the seat of their old car caught and pulled a thread in her suit and she swore, making Mr Saxby nervous. They had a lot to do that day: the bank, shopping, an Abbott and Costello picture.

They parked the car, and Mrs Saxby was glad to get going. She took Geoffrey with her to get him fitted with a new school uniform. He was starting high school soon, and had left Robert and their sister Eleanor far behind him. He had been given a wallet for Christmas, and a leather satchel. Mr Saxby watched them depart, turned back to Robert and Eleanor, and clapped his hands together. "Right. Let's see. Would you like to go exploring?"

In the last year of the war Robert had been only five years old and he could remember going by train into the city to meet his father back from the fighting. From the carriage window he had seen a football oval scored here and there with muddy trenches. There had been sand-bag walls around public buildings, striped with runnels of sand leaking from holes in the rotting bags. The post office had been battened down so that it looked like a fort.

Mr Saxby took them to see where he had scratched his

initials on the wall of a government building. They entered an alley. "I was on guard duty at the time and bored to bits," said Mr Saxby, standing awkwardly to obscure what Robert had already seen, "fuck" written at shoulder height and not easy to see unless you had wondered why your father was sidling along the wall while he talked to you. "That was before I got sent overseas," said Mr Saxby.

Later they all met for lunch in the cafeteria of the main department store. The other diners had the air of people after a change. They sat at the little tables, impatient with austerity now that the war was over. They were waited on by dark, silent Yugoslav women who had husbands driving graders somewhere up in the mountains or in the interior.

Mrs Saxby opened her handbag and took out a small fountain pen to make notes. She wrote some cheques and put them in envelopes and gave them to her husband. "On your way to the bank this afternoon could you drop these off?" she asked. "I'll do some shopping and take the kids to the pictures." Robert saw the apprehension on his father's face. He wondered what a bank manager could be like.

Their overcoats were hanging on a coat-stand near their table. A man in a dinner suit held their coats open and helped them put them on. Mr Saxby shook himself into optimism, clapped his hands and rubbed them together, and slapped a sixpence on the table. "Thank you for your gracious service," he said, offering the man another coin and gesturing, No, please don't do that, when the man gave a deep bow.

Mrs Saxby took the three children to the cinema by way of the busiest shopping streets so that they could look in the windows. She was alert for signs of the war but could not find any here. "But you just look along this lane," she said, taking them down a sunless little side street. They walked past a blighted patch of ground heaped with sandbags mucky with stains and weeds, and stopped in front of an abandoned tailor's shop. There was a bolt of drab cloth in the window, and a store dummy leaned against the glass, dressed in a cuff-less, lapel-less suit to which was attached a tag: "Victory Suit — 38 coupons". Some upstairs windows had been painted over or criss-crossed with strips of tarry paper. "It was very dangerous at night," she said, telling them about her best friend who had been knocked down by a car one night during a brown-out. "It was too dark to see properly, especially in winter in a fog."

They came out into the sunlight, their backs turned to side streets and the past, and marched into the cinema. At half past four they came out and waited for Mr Saxby. They watched him walk up the hill towards them, his hat pushed back and his hands in his pockets, holding himself upright even though leaning forward would have made his progress easier. He had undone the knot of his tie. He looked to be at odds with everything. "Well, looks like you're shickered," said Mrs Saxby brightly. He stopped and rubbed his face with both hands in a washing motion. "Might as well bloody be," he said. "No point in doing anything else."

They walked stiffly to the car to drive home. Robert sat in the back seat with Geoffrey and Eleanor. Eleanor, cross and tired, began squabbling with him about his elbow. "For Christ's sake, shut up the pair of you," said Mr Saxby, turning around and slapping their legs as they contorted to escape him.

"Hartley," warned Mrs Saxby.

Mr Saxby tooted his horn at someone. He put on the brakes, accelerated, braked again, so that their progress was jerky along the streets their mother had glowed upon two hours earlier. Near the business district a dark, clever-looking man got out of his car, looked straight at them, buttoned his ashy-grey suit coat over his white shirt and deep blue tie, reached into his car for a long, belted overcoat, fastened its buttons and belt, and drew fine black gloves from his pocket: wit and grace and certainty were on his face. Through the open window of their car at a traffic light, Robert heard the man's car door close like a secretive footstep on gravel.

"Just look at him," said Mr Saxby, who had been

burping and not saying pardon me. "Just look at him, would you? Bloody sis with his coat and gloves, thinks he's the ant's pants. Useless bloody silver-spooned mincing bastard. Just look at him. Oh dear, I do believe there's a teensy weensy bit of fluff on my sleeve. Oh, what a pity I have to park the *Jag* amongst all these people's cars. Well, what *shall* I do for the rest of the day? A sundowner with old Reg and Eric? Buy a painting? Squeeze a boy's bum?"

"Hartley," said Mrs Saxby. "I think that's quite enough."

3
Mrs Saxby

Robert's mother was not like other mothers, and the family was hard-pressed at times to keep up with her. You had to admire her energy and moral courage, and she did not suffer you gladly when you were foolish. In the kitchen in the mornings she snorted when she read the paper and let Mr Saxby and the children get their own breakfasts. Men with beards and women in slacks came around in the evenings to discuss Labor's prospects in the next election. Wanly observed by Mr Saxby, she spent hours laughing and talking over ideas with that Bill Prior bloke, her friend, the president of the local branch. Bill Prior was a man who winked and laughed.

And just when you had accustomed yourself to seeing little of her because she had thrown herself into Labor Party business, with all those meetings, overflowing ashtrays, leftovers for dinner, newspaper barriers at the breakfast table, long sessions of talk, wine and cheese with Bill Prior, she would turn around and envelop you with love, shock and please you with a vulgar intimacy, squeeze Mr Saxby somewhere naughty on their way out to a dinner or a ball, and kiss you goodnight in a rustling, dazzling black dress.

4
DESIRE, MEANNESS AND MADNESS

Mr Saxby had a large family and an automatic, unquestioning loyalty to it. "But I hate her," said Robert when Mr Saxby suggested that he might like to take Great-Grandma Saxby for a walk in the garden. "Do you?" replied Mr Saxby wonderingly, his face unused to the idea.

Great-Grandma Saxby came to Sunday lunch about once a month. Robert hated these visits. At the dinner table she released little farts and there was a strange, dull click in her jaw when she chewed mutton sliced up especially small for her by Mr Saxby. Robert did not like to sit beside his great-grandmother, but there was no escape for they were too small a family for evasion of duty, and in her lucid moments she insisted on it anyway. He calmly watched her, twisted up inside with hate and frustration, seeing those fluffing gases thinly working their way around the fat cheeks of her bottom to escape, hearing food creeping down through her wet red tubes, concocting in his mind the smells and moistures and substances caught in her crepitating underwear and creased old body. "I bought this roast at Simpson's, Grandma," bawled Mrs Saxby. "Do you remember Simpson's?" The old woman lifted a tiny pea on her fork, and when it fell off on to her plate she tried again, but it scooted down her bosom and she whimpered for it, hunted by ghost emotions. Deaf as a post.

"We're top-heavy with old people in this family," observed Mrs Saxby after one of these visits, waving her cigarette in the air, "and they're all indestructible."

Robert recognised the truth in this. He formed a picture of older people that was fashioned around their litanies of aches, the cold, the heat, the hours of lying awake the night before. Don't ever ask them how they've been feeling lately, he warned himself. On the other hand, if it was a duty visit and there were long minutes to fill, *do* ask them how they've been feeling lately. He could not escape or ignore them. His father had a large number of great-aunts, uncles and cousins, and Great-Grandma Saxby, and he was a man who did his duty. Mrs Saxby happily cooked and looked after them. She had long talks with them and had accumulated a frightening store of knowledge about the family.

She seemed to be the end point of her own family. She had a tired sister called Fay who wrote once a year from an unfamiliar town in another state, and there was also Auntie Joy who had married an American during the war and once sent Robert a baseball mitt. But their parents had died many years ago.

And so she made her husband's family her own. She sorted out the tangled who, where and when of the Saxbys, and put Fay's Christmas cards on a string looped under the mantelpiece. Her knowledge of Mr Saxby's family was deep and accurate, and she enriched it with plenty of accompanying motive, all nicely wicked and foolish as in a popular novel. Knowing the tugs and eddies of desire, meanness and madness gave her a knowing look at weddings and funerals. None of it mattered to her necessarily — it was all there for fashioning into a rich here-and-now. But Mr Saxby, on the other hand, who was closely defined by shadowy ancestors, brothers, uncles and grandfathers, all big, wealthy men, war heroes and landowners, was the kind of man who remained careless and ignorant of them all, and took them for granted, but could not be faulted if you happened to ask him if the king had any sisters or cousins.

5
NERVES

Robert was deliriously happy when, in a flourish of spending, his father went out and bought a white Holden Special. Business had improved and the bank had given Mr Saxby a loan. The family beamed. The war had been a persistent smudge on their lives since it had ended but now, amid the gloomy Austins, Humbers and pre-war Fords of their suburb, the new white Holden was like a visitor's car.

That weekend they went for a long drive. Mr Saxby's bracing manner at the front gate, and again when he got behind the steering wheel, told the family that they were setting out on a major expedition, but as soon as they got to the city's edge he breathed out heavily, slowed and stopped the car, and said, "I think you'd better drive, dear. I'm all right around the city, but I haven't got your eyes. I think you'll do much better than me on the open road."

Mrs Saxby drove like the men of those days drove, her elbow out the window and a cigarette streaming smoke from the other hand that rested negligently on the steering wheel. Robert enjoyed watching his mother lift a finger of acknowledgement to oncoming cars, and it became a private game with him to lean on the back of her seat and peer over her shoulder and count the number of responses she got.

He thought that this summer might be one of his happiest ever. He remembered those past holidays, when Mr Saxby had had to explain, in a voice penny-pinching and beguiling, that they could not afford to go away this year: "But you mustn't mind, we'll make the most of it, won't we? I'll make you a tree house. We'll go to the beach."

They played "Riddle me, riddle me, ree" for a while, and tested each other at adding up the numbers on registration plates. Mrs Saxby, as usual, chose strange examples and was the quickest adder. "Riddle me, riddle me, ree," she said, "I can see something that you can't see, and it starts with an N."

"'Nor,'" they said, Mr Saxby's pet name for Eleanor. "Needle on the petrol gauge. Nought on the speedo. Nut shells."

"Not even warm," said Mrs Saxby. "Nerves. Your father's nerves."

"I'm not nervous," said Mr Saxby quickly. "Do I look nervous to you kids?"

"What are you sitting like that for then," they said.

Mr Saxby took his hands out from under his thighs, sat back with his shoulder against the door and rested his arm along the back of the seat. His fingers brushed through the hair on his wife's shoulders. "I suppose you want us to have an accident," he said. "Two pairs of eyes are better than one, you know."

6
OPEN AND TRUSTING

Things improved. They moved to a bigger house, one that was suited to sprawling. Its buckled verandah faced a broad park where Mr Saxby liked to go and practise golf swings, and at the back of the house were a lichened fish pond and half an acre of tangled shrubs and old trained roses on trellises.

Inside the house Robert's footsteps on the wooden floors boomed around his ears and gathered near the high ceilings. He lay on his back in bed or on the lounge-room couch, watching faces emerge in the dampness stains on the ceiling and wondering how the rosettes stayed up. He fancied that there was a secret compartment somewhere and went about striking the dark panels with his knuckles. But there was a cellar out the back that had a tangled creeper over it which he lifted and let fall like a curtain behind him, leaving him in a soft, damp, stale-smelling room with shelves in it for his secret things, a dim, vegetable light illuminating everything.

Warm family reminiscing about the schools Mrs Saxby had taught in, Eleanor's memorable displays of bad temper, or the disastrous progression of Great-Grandma Saxby's senility, took place around the kitchen table on winter evenings. Mr Saxby often said, "There was a humdinger of a storm the night your mother had you, Rob." He slapped his knee. "I'd just come home on leave. Your mother thought we weren't going to make it because she'd used up her petrol ration. You were an ugly little bugger, all red and cross."

Every mother made egg-and-bacon pies in winter when Robert was growing up. They did not take long to make and were easily transported to a relative's house for a family dinner on a Sunday evening. On Saturday afternoons in winter Robert went with Mr Saxby and Eleanor to football games and got numbed by cold on far-away railway stations, waiting for a train home. A rattling of doors and fragments of strange conversations went with him across the dark, wet park between the station and the house, ebbing only when Mrs Saxby heaped his plate with a slice of pie. They could not afford a gas or an electric oven. They sat in the kitchen warmed by the old wood-burning stove, reminiscing, and just about anything might be funny. Afterwards they might sit around the fire in the lounge-room and Robert might be asked to read aloud to them. On reflection they agreed that he did *David Copperfield* best, especially the bits with Uriah Heep. Robert thought that he might become an actor.

The Saxbys bustled with people, pets and favourite objects. Kittens and an old stray dog tottered about the garden. There were some silkworms in a shoebox. Eleanor had her horse books, saddle and reins, and in the back garden Bluey and Curly hooked their claws into the wire netting of the aviary near the rose trellis. There were enamel plates on the back porch, their edges chipped and their sides flecked with dry milk and scabs of food. Moby Duck floated in the bath until his wooden bottom suppurated with soapy water like the paddle Mrs Saxby used for poking at clothes boiling in the copper.

Robert played in the garden and in the park, losing skin on tree trunks, asphalt and tin roofs. At school he got good marks. Cocky, successful, never quite graceful. He liked dogs. He thought that it might be nice to get a pup for Christmas. Dogs bounded about, open and trusting.

7
SONNY JIM

At least once a year Robert, Eleanor and Geoffrey visited Uncle Dave and Auntie Margaret on their farm, but this time Robert was to spend a week of the August school holidays there on his own. "Would you like that, dear?" his mother asked. Then she turned to Mr Saxby and said quietly, with a laugh, that with the kids home from school, with idle hands, it was understandable that Dave and Margaret had chosen just that time to shear the sheep.

Robert wanted to say something to her about his aunt and uncle's cold, cold house, about Auntie Margaret slapping his hand, or his cousins hiding from him and pushing him around, but he knew she would only reply, "Oh, I'm sure it wasn't as bad as all that," or "Next time they do it just punch them right back again."

They drove for two hours and arrived in time for lunch. Robert saw that his cousins had not changed much. They were still disagreeable: too big, too plain, too satisfied.

"Come here," they brayed after he had waved good-bye to his parents after lunch. They held him and pushed him a little, and he became entangled among them in one of the bedrooms. He did not perceive them as individual figures: the four of them seemed to move everywhere as one noisy organism with many destructive legs and arms. "Come here," they said, with a look of suppressing something important. "Now," said the biggest, waving one hand like a fist hiding something, "I'm going to rub this secret chemical on my hand and you got to tell me what it is." Robert bent down to the scratched and dirty palm, and instantly a fist slid down the callused skin and punched his nose.

"Dear, oh dear. Did they really," said Auntie Margaret in her kitchen, grinning into Robert's shocked, accusing face. "Well, I don't see any bones broken so you must be all right." She turned away from him and touched a wet finger to an iron that had been resting on a hot-plate of the wood-stove.

"You're getting fat, Sonny Jim," said Uncle Dave at lunch in the kitchen the next day. "Isn't he?" he said, turning to his wife. "Doesn't he look fatter to you?" They all turned to Robert and grinned. The sheep dogs groaned and stretched in their sleep on the chilly hearth, and Robert drew himself in a little because the room was so cold. Outside he could hear the sleety grey wind in the pine plantation on the hill.

"All the kids in this family have got daily chores to do," said Uncle Dave with a shout and a laugh as if he had just remembered. Robert's uncle was a rudely healthy man, not bothered by the cold, not bothered by the crusty bits of old food on his fork or the rim of his plate. Earlier Robert had been picking at something caught in the tines of his fork and had looked up to see his aunt watching him. "The dishes," said Auntie Margaret suddenly. The air was filled with congratulations: "Fatso can do the dishes."

The cousins took him to explore the pine plantation, the creek and the shearing shed, and Robert caught a lamb that had got out of a yard, so that was all right. There was an old house down the road where they met children from the other farms to do dirty things. They looked at some pictures and took some of their clothes off and pissed and shat a bit and then went home. Robert's new knowledge was awesome.

He inherited another job too, shutting up the hens at night so the foxes would not get them. "They're around at the moment," said Uncle Dave, "going after lambs weakened by this bloody cold."

At half-past ten Robert woke up and remembered the hens. He left the house and went to the chookhouse, remembering to walk wide of the woodheap in the dark. He got cold and wet and shut the wirescreen door, hearing one or two hens move in sleepy alarm. In the morning he wiped mud and dung off his slippers with a scrap of newspaper torn off the sheet folded at the bottom of the wardrobe in his room, and pushed it into a corner of his suitcase.

Tim was the baby of the family. "I saw Tim chasing the chooks yesterday," said Robert at breakfast. "I reckon what happened was they got scared and went and hid somewhere."

"Yes, but did you count them when you shut them up?" persisted Auntie Margaret. She let the hens out of the chookhouse every morning and collected the eggs.

"Sort of."

"How many?"

"Twenty-four, I think."

"Well, there couldn't have been. There are only sixteen there now, and bloody feathers all over the bloody yard."

Tim was rocked about in her arms in a passion and he dropped the finger of toast that he had been trying to eat. Auntie Margaret stopped rocking and wiped his mouth.

"Did you chase the chooks, Bub? Did you chase the chookies, my sweet?" she crooned on the top of his head. "You wouldn't do that, would you, precious." Tim suddenly smiled and offered her the top lopped from his boiled egg.

8
Puzzled and Out of Step

By Christmas Day in his tenth year Robert had conclusively proved to himself that Father Christmas did not exist. This made it easier for Mr and Mrs Saxby to produce the labrador pup, which Robert was to call Gypsy before the day was out. They gave Geoffrey a smart wristwatch, and Father Christmas brought Eleanor an English schoolgirls' annual, a horse book, ribbons for her hair, a gold bangle and a bone-handled brush-and-comb set. "We'll get some nice scraps of meat from Simpson's for Gypsy," said Mrs Saxby. "Feeding her will be your job, dear," she told Robert.

The day grew hotter. Mrs Saxby placed bamboo fans by the side-plates of the adults and put the butter dishes back in the fridge. Uncle Dave and Auntie Margaret and the four cousins were expected for lunch, but they were late. They finally arrived at one o'clock. "It's so hot out," they said. "The radiator boiled twice." Robert, Geoffrey and Eleanor, seated sourly on the rug by the unopened Christmas presents, glared up at their cousins trooping in the door. One of the cousins held his palm under Eleanor's nose. "Smell that," he said, and punched her. "Behave yourself, you kids," said Auntie Margaret, laughing immoderately.

"Hello, Ted old son," said Mr Saxby to his brother. "Bill," replied Uncle Dave. No-one knew why Hartley Saxby was called Bill, or why Dave Saxby was called Ted, or who started it. It annoyed everyone intensely. Robert kept himself on guard for any name that his father might want to start calling him.

"King's speech," said his father after lunch, looking from face to face. "King's speech everyone?"

"Yes," said Uncle Dave firmly. Auntie Margaret dabbed her napkin discreetly at the corners of her mouth. "That would be lovely," she said. Robert's mother muttered, "Waste of time if you ask me. I'm doing the dishes."

"Pat!" said Auntie Margaret in a shocked voice.

"It's time this country went its own way."

"I see," said Uncle Dave heavily. "Well, you can't tell me in those African places you have..."

"Don't waste your breath, Ted," said Mr Saxby. "Get her and bloody Bill Prior on that topic and you won't hear the bloody end of it."

The King's voice, sounding puzzled and irresolute, grew louder as the wireless valves warmed up. Mr Saxby held up his hand for quiet, a keen look of pleasure on his face. Uncle Dave leaned forward in an armchair, his hands between his knees rolling a flecked beer glass. He caught himself and humbly put down the glass. Auntie Margaret smiled at the crotchety children. In the kitchen the dishes rattled.

Mr Saxby waited until the speech and all postscripts were over and leaned to turn off the wireless. He began an involved conversation with Uncle Dave and Auntie Margaret about the King's relatives.

"He's not a well man," said Auntie Margaret.

The adults were lifted by the speech but slowed by the lunch. Dimly they became aware that the children had divided into hostile camps. "I'm hot," they wailed. "I want to go to the beach."

It seemed to take them hours to pack up and go. Robert waited. Suddenly, when no-one was looking, he hid a wheel from one cousin's present and strained the clockwork spring on another.

They went to the beach in two cars. Robert was humiliated because he was told to wear his underpants and give his cousin his bathers. Uncle Dave had a dusty waterbag hanging from the grille of his car. Robert drank from it avidly; he liked the fibrous taste but he was careful to avoid the scum marks on the china cork-hole. One cousin watched him, ready to pounce with derision if he should wipe it on his shirt. The heat made Robert feel sluggish and he needed to drink. He thought of Gypsy, soft and golden, lying on the cement verandah where it was cool.

The adults spread two army blankets on the sand and the children went away to swim and make forts. It seemed to Robert that the whole city had come to the beach. He was certain of that fact when he saw some kids he knew at school. His cousins had stopped being nasty and were asking him to imagine the women's bodies under their bathers. The children huddled together, their feet in a pool, watching a group of older kids flirting. The girls pulled forward the tops of their bathers and peered inside and giggled, and the boys seemed to want to wrestle with the girls. The larking got more frantic and Robert and his cousins followed them into the sea. "What do you kids want?" said a boy with his arm around a girl's waist.

They wandered back to the adults. "Where's Eleanor?" said Mrs Saxby.

Robert felt hot with alarm. "Somewhere," he said, looking around.

They were sent off to search and found Eleanor crying, blindly stumbling between two women holding her hands. Robert claimed her and took her back to Mrs Saxby. "Weren't you a silly duffer," said Mrs Saxby, folding Eleanor's hot face into her brown shoulder. "Hey," announced Uncle Dave, his open legs allowing Robert a glimpse of a wrinkled pouch of grey skin with a blue vein running through it, "young Rob's got underpants on! Fatso's got his undies on."

9
A Mulish Look

Gypsy rarely walked a straight line, and when she was lectured or slapped, she wagged her tail, ready to play. "Hello, Dopey," Robert's father would say, pulling at her golden ears. "You're a real dope, Dopey."

But everyone was fed up with this constant business of calling things by the wrong name. "Her name's Gypsy," said Mrs Saxby finally. "Everyone else calls her Gypsy. No one calls her Dopey. People who visit don't know what you mean when you say Dopey. Gypsy herself gets confused. Gypsy's name is Gypsy and has been ever since we got her. She's not your dog. Gypsy."

Mr Saxby gently boxed the foolish black snout resting on his knee and adopted a mulish look. "She looks dopey," he said. "She acts dopey."

10
EYES OPENED

"I'm sorry, dear," said Mrs Saxby, "but she's your pet and you must take some of the responsibility for her."

Simpson's butcher's shop was on the corner of their street, about five minutes' walk away. On hot afternoons after school Robert grizzled his way out of the house and slammed the wire gate behind him. The sun seemed to hang just above the back of his head. It melted the asphalt into patches that stuck in bruising knots on the soles of his sandals. On hot days the walk to Simpson's was long, all for a few blarmy bones. And then he had to turn around and come back again, flies and neighbours' dogs catching at the scent.

Gypsy swallowed the flaps of meat and fat that he dropped for her, her jaws shutting with a click. She took her bones away to chew and bury. The Jackson children from next door hung over the fence, shooting cherry pips at her with a catapult and idly jeering at Robert. "Cut it out," he said. "You might hit her in the eye."

They climbed into the yard and he played with them for a while. His feelings towards them were faintly disapproving and apprehensive. They were a brother and sister with unstable faces and quick, darting strength. They had learned their violence from their father, a singleted man who threatened to thrash Gypsy if he found her in his yard again. He once lost a row with Mrs Saxby about his burning rubbish on a washing day; he banged back into his house, tongue-tied with fury, wearing only underpants and boots. He had an engineless car out in the street, and two more resting on their axles in long grass in the backyard, the children playing in them while bantam hens and chicks pecked about. In a shed in the back corner, two greyhounds whined.

"Your car's a bomb," the Jackson children would say to Robert. "Your dog isn't a pedigree like ours." In Robert's mind they were like all the others: the gang of stand-over boys at school who sometimes pulled down Eleanor's pants, the four Saxby cousins who poked and jabbed, their mouths open. Robert hated the way all these children laughed, sated and triumphant. He hated their mothers and fathers for their clannishness and indifference.

But then there might be a reversal, and he might be invited next door to play. Mrs Jackson made tomato sauce, apricot jam, chutney, pickles, butter, ice-cream and ginger beer. She wiped her hands on her dress or her shapeless cardigan that had a hole in each elbow and crustings at the wrists. Once Robert was invited to stay for a night and his eyes were opened.

11
A HIGH COLOUR

Mrs Saxby needed room to sprawl. She scattered her papers and books about, and her friends sprawled after meetings, drinking wine and beer and talking about the Party's difficulties. Bill Prior held court from a cushion on the hearth and stayed behind after all the others had gone home. Robert kept to his own room while all this was going on and Mr Saxby sat in the lounge-room corner by the sewing basket.

Soon Bill Prior was dropping by twice a week with a bottle of beer, to chat or go over some issue for the next Branch meeting with Mrs Saxby. Bill Prior poured a glass of beer for Robert. "Come on," he said. "Won't hurt you. Had my first glass when I was your age." Robert looked to his father, whose face always became expressionless whenever Bill Prior visited, but Mr Saxby was uncomforting, turning away as though he could not be bothered with anyone. Mrs Saxby had a high colour and waited with a cheerful laugh. Robert raised the glass to drink from it. It was foul, the smell catching high in his nostrils.

12
A Twist of Repulsion

If anyone asked him what he wanted to do when he left school, Robert would never list teaching. Whenever it was suggested, he felt a twist of repulsion.

He did not want to be like his mother, who carried her teaching notes around in a child's cardboard school case, and after dinner sat on the floor in front of the fire to correct compositions, wheezing through her final Craven A for the day. Privately he was pleased that small children yelled, "Hello, Mrs Saxby" to his mother across busy streets, or held her hand to tell her things, but he did not want to be like her.

He did not want to be like the little man who strolled away from the blackboard to knock boys' heads with a chunky signet ring and say, "Well, Sunshine?", or the frightened girl in a dust-coat who one day screamed and threw one piece of chalk after another at him, or his grey-faced history teacher in the suit with enormous lapels who talked with dreadful relish about "behind the Iron Curtain".

Nor did Robert want to be like his father, who called things by the wrong name and who dreamed of publishing but was stuck with printing wedding invitations for all and sundry, and Labor Party newsletters for Bill Prior, a man he did not like. Robert did not want to be like his sister, who thought that her beautiful hair would see her through, or like Geoffrey, with his long fingers unused to sunshine or dirt, or his cousins, who were always ready with pinching, punching torments.

13
IDENTIFYING TAGS

For each of her children, Mrs Saxby performed tiny services that were like private identifying tags. She gave Geoffrey a matching fountain pen and propelling pencil for his seventeenth birthday, and for Christmas thick bond paper in a leather slip-case. Sometimes Robert was expected to help Mr Saxby clean up the printing shop after school while Geoffrey sat home at his desk, the fountain pen in one hand and with perhaps a smear of blue ink on one bloodless knuckle. Robert came home for dinners, his fingers stained from cleaning printing plates with a wire brush and solvent. He complained. "But this is an important year for Geoffrey," said Mrs Saxby. "You wouldn't want him to fail, would you?"

Eleanor's hair was thick, the colour of wheat, and Mrs Saxby never tired of admiring it or tying it up with ribbons, or letting it fill out like smoke over her shoulders. Eleanor brushed her hair with a hundred strokes a day, and it crackled and lifted lazily to the brush.

Robert read to the family around the fire on winter nights, practising his heartfelt Heathcliff voice and his oily Uriah Heep hands, and at school he trembled in the wings of the hall stage. Mrs Saxby told him that she thought he was the most creative of her children. She showed him how to write his signature so that it looked confident and interesting, and she took him aside to say, "All's fair in love and war" after his heart was broken in his second year at the high school.

Meanwhile Robert's father had become a man who did his best to enjoy life and involve his children as well. He became a vigorous, ineffectual man in the water or on a tennis court or playing field. He shouted commentaries on the state of play and warned of his intentions. His teammates, partners and children neatly dodged him, going on with the game and letting him clap them across the shoulders afterwards. It was said of Mr Saxby that he was not much use but he livened things up.

In summer the four of them watched Test cricket from grass mounds. As a spectator Mr Saxby was quite unlike his sporting self; he sat quietly and contentedly, sometimes making notes in the margins of his programmes. In the train afterwards he would ask them questions like, "Did you notice how their scoring dropped after they made that position change?" Mr Saxby told his children that having speed and grace — and he did not deny for a minute that they did have them — was all very well, but you needed to think like a tactician as well. "You need the theory and you need the practice," he said.

But there is always going to be someone who says that you need the killer instinct, and nothing else matters. This bothered Robert and one day he asked, "Dad, what about the killer instinct? That's what Mr Prior reckons you need."

Instantly Mr Saxby's serious, helpful face turned private and subdued. "Let's hope there's more to it than that, son," he said. He turned away to finish painting a white line representing the height of a tennis net on the brick wall of the garage. Over his shoulder he said, "You're a natural, son. That's all that's needed."

They walked across the road to the park and Mr Saxby showed him how to stroke from Bradman's cricket book. On summer evenings before a Test match Eleanor and Robert sat with Mr Saxby at the kitchen table working out fielding positions on butcher's paper with a yellow crayon. Mrs Saxby would sit watching them, her eyes screwed up against the smoke from her cigarette, and then she might get up and phone Bill Prior about a matter of Branch business.

And so Robert grew to have a placid, indistinct sense of himself. He had fine, sometimes tragic passions, but never quite managed to find the right occasion for revealing them.

14
INJUSTICE

On a Friday afternoon after cricket practice Robert came home from school, dumped his bag in his room, and found his mother standing in the kitchen, tense and solicitous. "You'd better have a look at Gypsy," she said, keeping Eleanor in the kitchen with her.

Five minutes later she came out to him on the verandah, where he was squatting down next to Gypsy on the cool, glassy cement between the geraniums in their pots. "She's been a naughty girl apparently," said Mrs Saxby.

Robert felt the horror and the injustice. He looked up at his mother, away from Gypsy's cut face stretched cheerless between her paws. "No, dear," said Mrs Saxby, seeing his face, "you know I wouldn't hurt her. She got in next door and made a mess of their garden — which is rather a joke in itself — and ate three of the chickens. Mr Jackson gave her a thrashing. I heard it." She leaned down with him, Gypsy's pitiful eye rolling to follow her. "Poor old thing," she said, putting out her hand and resting her fingers between Gypsy's ears. The tip of Gypsy's tail rose and fell.

Robert could not think about the stones and sticks and Mr Jackson's boots and his spit flying. He was struck by an image of Gypsy escaping, of her limping and scuttling in pain past the side of the house next door and onto the gravel path, squeezing in terror through the gate, puffing along the footpath, her poor paws hurting her, yelping in shock and shame at their front gate to be let in, her tongue dripping. Her face had always been so pleased and curious about everything that went on. She didn't know.

Robert ran over to the fence dividing the houses and kicked it. He leaped for the top rail, lifting his face over it. Mr Jackson was scratching his leg, idly looking at the fence.

"You bloody bastard, leave my dog alone," Robert yelled.

Mr Jackson turned to go inside, dismissing Robert with a wave of his hand and saying, "A bloody mongrel of a useless prick of a fucking dog. I bloody told you, right?" He scattered a cigarette butt with a twist of his thick sole. His two children ran out into their yard to confront Robert. "Don't you call our father a bastard," said the girl. "Our father said your dog's a bloody nuisance and should be shot," said the boy.

The three children began a fight with clods of dirt from their gardens. "Now stop that this minute, Robert," said Mrs Saxby. "You're only falling to their level." She made him accompany her back to the verandah.

"Bloody bathtub, bloody bathtub," chanted the Jackson children. Mrs Saxby rubbed Robert's back until he felt loved.

He waited until there was a holiday weekend. Using Mrs Saxby's typewriter, he pecked out letters to the police and a landscape gardener, and ran down to the mailbox outside Simpson's to post them. He had to hurry; the family had been invited to Uncle Dave's for three days. The Jacksons next door had already left to visit one of "our grans" or "our aunties" they were always talking about. Robert imagined surly grandmothers and aunts with Jackson faces, standing in aprons in gardens in mean towns far away.

The Saxbys got back late on Monday night. On Tuesday morning, when Robert left for school, he saw that the Jacksons were still away. Robert arrived home from school at four o'clock. Mr Jackson was explaining something to a policeman who had his hand on the raised bonnet of the engineless car that Mr Jackson was going to do up one day. "I'd say it's been here longer than that," the policeman was saying. Gravel from two loads dumped in Mr Jackson's front garden was spilling through the fence onto the footpath. "Must be going to do some work on the place," said Mr Saxby at dinner that evening.

15
Drama and Regard

When Gypsy got skittled by a car a few months later, they buried her in the back yard by the mulch heap. Robert marched up and down the grave in his rubber boots, flattening the soil, feeling noble in bereavement.

His father had disappeared inside the gardening shed. He came out with a small pine slab. He tapped it into the compacted soil, the pointed end searching out Gypsy's head somewhere below as the back of the axe fell. A long splinter almost peeling off bisected the large letter *D* that he had carved with a chisel. He smoothed back the splinter with his thumb and a kind of obstinate pride. "Hart," said Mrs Saxby, "take it out again and let Robert put something of his own there. Why do you do these things? I don't know."

Robert made his own stake, tacking to it a weathered piece of cardboard on which he had written "Gypsy" in red ink. Within a week Mr Saxby was saying, "I miss that dog. That dog we had wouldn't have hurt a fly."

During the next few years they bought a little terrier that growled at them from armchairs, the cats went away to die, and the budgies were sold to someone at school. Eleanor still yearned to own a horse. But Robert stopped thinking of pets; pets were simply things that people had around the house somewhere.

16
Out of Turn

The English teacher got them to read aloud from *David Copperfield*, taking a paragraph each in turn. Somebody's pencil rattled and voices came from distant classrooms.

Robert sat insensible to everyone in the room, imagining, exultant and despising, how he might play Uriah Heep, his snaky twistings, his wiping the palms of his damp-fish hands with a handkerchief, his knowing his umble station. A slow boy struggled with a passage, completing it with relief. Into the short pause that followed, Robert's voice took up the story — loud, out of turn, and dripping with Uriah Heep's unction. He wrung his hands and snaked in his seat.

Gradually Robert became aware of the boy next to him poking him. He stopped reading and looked up. Thirty boys and girls and a teacher were ogling him, their faces open-mouthed and gleeful. Robert blushed. The teacher led the laughter and as abruptly ended it with sharp raps of his ring on his desk.

Robert knew this man well. Last month the school had been hushed with scandal: a boy from a lower form had been cuffed with the ringed hand, there had been a bruise, some blood and headaches. The father, dressed in an ill-fitting suit, curling his hat brim in his well-scrubbed hands, came to protest. Robert was bell monitor that month, a task that let him roam in critical places. He saw Mr Coupe sitting neglected in a corridor. Forty minutes later he came back to ring the bell for lunch: the corridor was empty and Robert walked along it wriggling his shoulders as if to make them comfortable inside an unfamiliar suit coat, kneading a hat brim between his workman's thumb and forefinger. Teachers materialised ahead of him in the corridor, on each other's heels in the doorway of the Staff Room. Robert heard a voice: "We sent the bastard packing with a flea in his ear."

17
A New Man

Now that business had improved, Mr Saxby piled the family into the car and they set off down the coast for a holiday, to spend two weeks in a hotel in a small town.

There was a plank swinging from chains above the driveway entrance to the hotel, announcing that this was "Culloden". The main building needed a new coat of paint and the flyscreens on the windows sagged with rust. They went inside, where Mr Saxby registered. The kind of bossy girl who wears jodhpurs and has a horse to feed and comb and obviously belongs to the place gave Robert uncivil directions to the path that led to the beach. When he got to his bedroom, Robert wet his hair in an effort to get it to sit down at the back; but after less than two days of the girl's displeased face and her indifference to Eleanor, who also loved horses, Robert gave up all thoughts of love. Eleanor and Geoffrey were much better company and they had two weeks of beach ahead of them.

Their father was a bit silly the way he behaved like a big kid. Your own father. It was embarrassing to find him running or yelling or tackling you, his feet kicking up the sand behind him; but he was a new man compared to this time last year, and in a much better mood on holiday than he was at home. Mrs Saxby seemed to change along with him. They were like a couple of lovebirds the way they kissed and cuddled, daring the kids to protest.

Mr Saxby went for a swim at six o'clock on their first morning at the hotel, but during breakfast he wrapped himself in his arms and said never again. He exchanged a smile with Mrs Saxby. Every morning after that the children ate alone, coming into the dining-room at seven o'clock, peering through the quiet orange light that was pin-pricked with dust motes, looking with interest at the other families and children choosing cereals and jams from the long table near the door.

At lunch, Mr Saxby would be full of life. "Now, don't wander off," he would say. "We'll play cricket this afternoon and go for a walk. All right? We'll do family things," he said.

In the evenings they showered, changed their clothes and had drinks on the hotel verandah. A drinks waiter got to know them and, without being asked, brought Robert and Eleanor drinks made of different coloured layers. They saw the sun settle into the sea a long way away. "This is the life," said Mr Saxby. "Isn't this the life, kids?"

Two days before they were due to go home Robert came back along the sand from a walk in search of caves. In an idle fashion he pulped jellyfish with a stick, sighed heavily from time to time, saw a longboat from a privateer beach itself and attacked and repelled the landing party with his sword. And, when he turned down a slope of a sand-dune and saw Mr and Mrs Saxby lying together kissing, his mother's hand inside his father's bathers, both of them wrought up with some kind of fervent strain, he knew he had found an explanation for his strange feeling of lack these past weeks.

They did not see him. The next day he found reasons to stay at their sides all day. By shower-time they were a little annoyed with the ardour of his attentions, the games he wanted to play with them, the favours he offered, his bright eagle-eyes looking at them. Geoffrey, wandering past with Robert's camera, took a photograph of Robert scooping up sand to bury them.

18

SHADOWS CONTORTED

Mr and Mrs Saxby lived in mettlesome community with one another, or in silence, but now Robert was aware of the flow of looks and touches that sometimes connected them. He remembered his mother unfolding a globey breast when Eleanor was a baby; he took note of her alarming beauty when she dressed in black to go to a ball, and of his father's charmed eye.

They were immoderate, they embarrassed him, but he was drawn to them. He liked to sit at the kitchen table to do his homework in the evening, writing his essays, drawing his graphs, and daydreaming, but between seven o'clock and half-past seven he sat tense, almost without breathing, as Mr and Mrs Saxby cleaned up and washed the dishes. He tried to ignore the noises — slaps, giggles, the tea-towel flipped at his mother's bum, the bar of soap spurting from her hands, a sloppy kiss, their delighted laughs and shouts as they stacked dishes and threw the cutlery into the drawers — but the noises were always punctuated with sudden periods of quiet in which he thought he could hear the softest noise or whisper. He turned around sometimes and once saw them standing forehead to forehead, one hand behind the other's head, their hips a little apart to allow room for the other hand. Mostly they stood side by side, their arms around each other, looking peacefully out of the window at their shadows contorted on the wall of shrubs outside.

At other times Robert didn't know what to think. Mrs Saxby might suddenly say, "Things change between a man and a woman when they've lived together for a long time." She would sit with her elbow on the table, her neck arched, dribbling smoke into the air. "You'll learn," she said, "that where love is concerned, kindness is more important than honesty." Robert turned to look at Mr Saxby sitting there with his glass of sherry and the evening paper, and wondered if he had heard her and, if he had, did he mind?

19
LAST MINUTE

Traditionally the family slept in on Sundays, but not quite so long this time because breakfast-in-bed had to be made for Mrs Saxby and they had to watch her open her presents, half of which hadn't been wrapped yet. Theirs was a last-minute sort of household.

Bill Prior called by for a short time in the afternoon with six yellow roses. He came to see Mrs Saxby two or three times a week. He winked and he laughed. He was the kind of man who beats an undeflecting path when it comes to bringing roses to a married woman in the heart of her lounge-room, husband and children. Bill Prior, nodding to them left and right, was soon at the side of Mrs Saxby, who stood in front of the log fire with the back of her skirt hoisted. Eleanor hurried into the kitchen for a vase, and Robert and his father watched as one old friend gave the other a kiss. Mrs Saxby looked moved.

After Bill Prior had left they started cooking. Some of the family were coming to dinner and, while Mrs Saxby put her feet up, Mr Saxby drove somewhere in the Holden, Robert went next door for some mint, Eleanor rolled pastry, and Geoffrey supervised, running his long white forefinger along the labels on the herb and spice tins in a row on a pantry shelf. Mr Saxby came back at five o'clock, disappeared somewhere, and then joined them in the kitchen.

Robert, on his way through to the china cabinet, was stopped by the scent and abundance of twenty-four red long-stemmed roses in a vase, a tiny card at the base saying to my lovely, lovely wife. Mrs Saxby wandered in soon after that, there was a commingling of husband and wife, assurances that really red was her favourite colour, but Bill meant well.

20

WITHDRAWAL

Then there was that snapping hot week when the Saxbys and Bill Prior and his family drove to a high-gabled guest-house in the mountains for a holiday. But something wasn't right: from the moment the two cars arrived, Mrs Saxby seemed to close up and hide herself away. At lunch time she was late coming into the dining room; Mr Saxby stood and smiled and pulled a chair out for her. "I can manage," she said. At six o'clock, when Robert was exploring the stairs and corridors, waiting for the dinner gong to sound, he heard her voice in the library: "I'm finding it difficult. This was not a good idea." A voice replied; she was talking to Bill Prior. Robert walked into the library saying, "I wish the gong would go for dinner." His mother said instantly, "You're always around, aren't you, Robert?"

The next day she hid in a cavernous armchair like a discarded great-aunt, her books and cigarettes on a chrome and bakelite ashtray-stand beside her. She seemed to find it an effort to talk. Every day after that, if they sought her out for a hike or a game of tennis, she would not look up until the cajoling or sulking got too much for her, and then they would see a baffling pain in her eyes. She backed away from them into her books and a great lassitude settled upon her. Robert watched her fearfully, seeing her talk to Bill Prior with her eyes.

Mr Saxby panicked. Trembling with courage in the face of her withdrawal, he became a raconteur at mealtimes, leaped for impossible tennis balls with his racquet, charmed old ladies, and dallied with the less risky of the two waitresses, one eye always on Mrs Saxby. Robert looked at his curious parents and filed the details away.

Eventually Bill Prior announced, with a look of embarrassment and regret on his face, that he and his family were cutting their holiday short. Something had come up at home and they'd better be on their way. "That's a shame," said Mr Saxby, standing behind Mrs Saxby's chair, resting his hands on the back of it.

No-one seemed constant on that holiday. Robert sat in a glowing corner of the dining room in the mornings, under a stained glass window, spooning marmalade from a filigreed silver bowl, avoiding the awful eyes of a stag at bay on the wall nearby, feeling displaced. And, without knowing why one waitress was risky and the other not, Robert knew that his father would never gamble with the risky waitress for that might be too certain of succeeding, and yet a rebuff from her would matter too much as well. Robert saw, finally, a plea in his mother's eyes, *Let me be*, but no-one else seemed to see it; and another plea, *It's not you, Hart, it's not you, dear*, which his father did not see because he believed that it *was* him. All these things Robert knew without knowing what to do with them or how to describe them, supposing someone should have sat him down to question him about it.

21
Cultural Wing

When Robert turned fifteen Mr Saxby said he thought he was now old enough to earn himself some regular money during the holidays. "The job's there if you want it, son," he said. And so, apart from two weeks in which the whole family set off on a caravan trip, Robert spent the hot weeks of December and January in his father's printing shop. He had sold newspapers in the past, picked weeds out of gardens, washed cars, but had never worked alongside people before.

"We owe these people something, son," said Mr Saxby. "It's not easy coming to a new country." He had four men working for him: Miklos, the work-obsessed senior man, Thomas his jolly friend, Ferdinand called Fred, and Len the apprentice. "I tell you what, these blokes know more about printing than I'll ever know," said Mr Saxby. Apart, that is, from Len, who chain-smoked in a sly, hurried way, admired certain singers, and drew a plastic comb from the back pocket of his blue jeans, using it to pull back his hair before shattering the suburban streets on his heavy motorbike, his girlfriend clutching onto his back. At the workshop, Len exasperated Miklos, Thomas laughed through the days, and Fred was as morose and silent as an anarchist who cannot come to a decision.

The local merchants and citizens were expansive and confident and the orders poured in. Mr Saxby printed the football team's season's programme with blank spaces for the scores, the timber yard wanted leaflets for its annual sale, the high school ordered six hundred sporting certificates, enough for the next few years, everyone knew that Mr Saxby could do gold embossing on invitation cards, and Bill Prior had a long-standing arrangement for Mr Saxby to print any local Labor Party material.

Mr Saxby guided Robert between the presses, cans of ink and boxes of type, saying, "Through here, mind that lever," and stood with him before Miklos's bench, a beneficent smile on his face, his fingers entwined. Miklos made a point of finishing setting a line of type before he looked up. He was an unsmiling, precise man and made Robert feel nervous.

"Now this is Mr Novotny, Rob, you've met him before. He's going to show you his side of things this week, then next week Thomas will take you in hand, and after that we'll see what happens."

Robert saw that his father was babbling on in the face of Miklos Novotny's stare. Miklos had a lot to do, his fingers were itching to dig into the box of type on his bench.

Mr Saxby wound down, there was something he had to do before he forgot, and he hoped Rob would listen and watch carefully. He backed away with a smile, knocking his elbow on a lever, his voice losing itself in the thick smell of ink and paper. "You watch me finish," said Miklos, and Robert rushed through the week at Miklos's side. He had an uneasy feeling of irrelevance, the boss's son with two left feet, unhandy and unneeded but who had to be put up with.

The first two or three mornings' smokos were enchanting. The presses were shut off, there were no more hands reaching to make adjustments, and the four men and Robert cleaned their hands on cotton waste and sank onto the floor, their silent tools and metal plates gathering a patina of inky stillness.

On the first morning Robert watched for what he should do. Len never ate anything, he noticed; he just chain-smoked and joked and made vulgar noises, drinking his tea, black and sweet, straight from his flask. Every day Thomas's wife packed him rich cakes which he broke and passed around. Miklos ate black bread, cheese and salami for morning and afternoon smokos and lunch. Fred could not keep still. He walked to the park, the library, the shops.

Miklos, Thomas and Len would not say anything for the first few minutes. They sat, collapsed, slowly eating their food and rolling their cigarettes. Bit by bit one of them might say something and it would be responded to, or an argument might start; they might ask Robert's opinion or praise him for something, or Len might ask him to fetch a left-handed hammer because you are more or less obliged to have a go at the boss's son; Miklos might snap when Len's baiting got too thoughtless or confident, or a joke might be made that Robert felt certain concerned his father or himself. But he was powerless to understand or do anything about it, and the minutes would pass in a routine foreign to Robert but full of mystery and promise.

Mr Saxby had a project in mind. He swept into the shop one day in a fever; even Miklos's eyes lit up. Apparently there was a man, a carpenter, under the cultural wing of Mrs Saxby and Bill Prior, who liked to scribble away in the evenings when he was not patting down the tobacco in the bowl of his pipe during Branch meetings. Some of his stories had found their way into print here and there. "He writes from life," said Bill Prior. "He celebrates, but he's also got something sharp and truthful to say." Mrs Saxby was the first to suggest a book of the best of the man's stories, nicely printed and bound, sold by subscription. Mr Saxby glowed at the idea. Here was something he had been wanting to do for years.

Robert cleaned ink off metal plates with a wire brush, watching his father and Miklos in a huddle over paper, dimensions, typefaces and a dust jacket for the book. The carpenter was shown around. At home, Robert's mother and Bill Prior made their story selection and the carpenter was brought in for the final say. He was a man who took his pipe away from his mouth only briefly to offer his opinions.

But over the weeks Robert observed them all lose their energy, the little flare-ups in the hot weather, his father washing his hands of the whole thing. Miklos and Mr Saxby were united in condemning the author, who hovered at the side of Miklos's work bench, asking for changes to his stories, offering new stories, or suggesting a different order for them, the artist in him stirred into a hunger at the possibilities. Some pages were printed; Bill Prior pointed out that the paper was too thin, the ink showed through. A thousand dust jackets were printed and stacked into a box and forgotten while all this was going on. And besides, a large order from the Shire Council had come in so the book simply had to wait a while. "It wouldn't be a good idea to rush it," said Mr Saxby. Probably he was disappointed that his pet project could not go ahead just yet but, at the same time, he seemed to be above all the silly posturing that was going on and had better things to do. One day they received a letter from the carpenter saying he had gone to the country for three months and, meanwhile, here were two more stories, new ones, which he thought they would agree were better than some of the others in the book. School started again in February and Mr Saxby was busy.

Robert went back to the printing shop in the May school holidays. Mr Saxby asked him to find somewhere in the back room for the box of dust jackets because it was getting in everyone's way. Now and then he would say, "Perhaps I'll see it through sometime towards the end of the year. Or perhaps next year."

22
On His Way

Aunt Alice came over by bus to help out three days a week. She was useful around the house, made sure that

Robert and Eleanor were not growing out of their school uniforms and worked three half-days doing Mr Saxby's accounts. Having as many members of his family around as possible made Mr Saxby's face beam. Mrs Saxby was pleased to let Auntie Alice take over the shopping and cooking from time to time because she had a lot on her mind, especially Labor Party business. Between meetings she absent-mindedly played with Eleanor's hair, and she liked to say to Auntie Alice that she never darned socks when it was easier to buy them.

And so it was left to Auntie Alice and Mr Saxby to notice Robert's shiny pants seat, gaping pockets, pimples, emergent ankles and wrists, and top buttons in danger of popping off. They found a second-hand school uniform advertised in the newspaper, and Auntie Alice poured into Robert's drawers and wardrobe things that he could not bring himself to wear. She complained if she saw him in his old jeans and hand-knitted jumpers, and he had to assure her that he kept her presents for best. "I wear them to parties and things, Auntie Alice," he said, "or when I take my girlfriend to the pictures."

"What's her name?" said Auntie Alice, but then Robert was saved from a tangle of invented details when she said, "She's not a Catholic, I hope." Soon she was off and running.

Meanwhile Mrs Saxby's mind was far away as usual, but she did grow aware that Robert was flourishing. She sometimes edged past him shyly in the kitchen, and she once gave him an expensive razor with an abrupt air of ceremony, as though launching him on his way.

"I wonder if you'll go bald like your father," she said. Robert's voice squeaked and she giggled fondly. She noticed the squeak but not his clothes. Her laugh was a kind of delighted appreciation of him. It was like the laughs she reserved for Bill Prior's jokes.

23
WASHED OUT

Auntie Alice would not ask a neighbour to wind her kitchen clock for her, oh no, not her, and consequently she had a bad fall, broke her arm, and was staying with the Saxbys until she got stronger. "Eh?" she said, leaning forward and cupping her ear. "I didn't quite catch that, dear." She made her own dresses and they hung on her like cassocks. She took out the white handkerchief that she kept tucked under the dull copper bracelet on her wrist and wiped her eyes. She loved being with the family and laughed often, making her eyes water. "When am I going to meet your girlfriend, dear?" she asked Robert. "What girlfriend?" said Mrs Saxby.

Robert heard Auntie Alice get up at five o'clock every morning and sit on the verandah outside his bedroom window with a cup of tea. He knew that she saw the best part of the day, when cotton shirts feel wonderful for an hour or so, the light grows stronger, the soft air grows gently warmer and the clean smells of the night are still present. Robert knew that it would be a nice gesture to sit with her — she would not expect him to talk much, that was for meal-times and evenings when she went on and on — but he only got as far as beating his pillow with his fist as if to say, I don't feel up to it, before he turned over again and went back to sleep.

By lunchtime Mrs Saxby would have let down all the canvas blinds on the sunny side of the verandah. They had lunch in the kitchen, the sunlight coming in between a blind-edge and the verandah post, making streaks of brightness that cut through the dim kitchen air. The oven made the room too hot, and there were more suitable places to sit, but everyone socialised in the kitchen. In here Mrs Saxby held her informal chats with Bill Prior and the other branch members as they arrived, testing the ground for what was hidden, before she started the meeting in the living-room.

At lunchtime Auntie Alice would fan herself with a Japanese fan that Mr Saxby had brought home with him from the war. She ate tiny amounts very slowly, talking about the family with Mrs Saxby. Mr Saxby would offer to slice her cold meat for her. "No, dear," she would say. "That's all right." Robert sat opposite her and daydreamed, sometimes exchanging secret smiles with his mother at the things Auntie Alice said.

"I saw Mervyn Hall the other day," said Mr Saxby one day. "Auntie Alice, I saw Mervyn Hall the other day."

Auntie Alice patted at her eyes. She said: "Is he still no good? He broke poor Noel's heart."

"That's nonsense, Auntie Alice. What on earth are you talking about?"

Auntie Alice put her good hand on the edge of the table as though playing a chord and her fingers moved fretfully.

"Noel Hall and I grew up together. He was a lovely boy, he always made me laugh. My father said the Halls were drinkers, but Noel was a good boy. He could ride any horse you showed him. I was only twenty then; that was fifty years ago. We were going to get married but my father said no. Noel went away. I've never forgotten him. He married Elsie Hirschausen and Mervyn was born, but it wasn't a happy family; he told me about it."

By now she was crying and Robert thought, Oh Godfather.

"I've never forgotten him," said Auntie Alice. "I've never looked at another man."

Robert gave an elaborate yawn. Auntie Alice kept crying and he rolled his eyes at his mother, but she said, "That's quite enough, my boy," and turned to put her arm around Auntie Alice.

Robert knew that he had been nasty, but he sulked for the rest of the day. Auntie Alice was washed out by seven o'clock when they sat down to eat dinner, her voice fading away at the ends of her sentences. Mrs Saxby raised one or two family names but Auntie Alice did not follow them up. She looked reproachfully at Robert once, and a few minutes later said, "You're a good boy, dear," when he picked up her ebony napkin ring from the floor.

Later, when they were having a cup of tea before the washing up, Uncle Dave walked in saying, "It's only me. Thought I'd see how you were getting on, Auntie Alice." He was in town to pick up a tractor part.

"They looking after you all right, old girl?" he shouted.

He gave her a loud kiss and she brightened. "Dave," she said. "Darling Dave. You're a good boy."

Uncle Dave soon had Auntie Alice laughing about something his neighbour had done. "Take me home with you, dear," she said. "I want to go home with you."

Robert was to remember looking across the table at Auntie Alice and snarling, "No, Uncle Dave. She's not strong enough yet. She has to stay here."

24

DISCOVERED

When Robert was sixteen the Jackson girl next door suddenly died from a brain tumour. The next day their class teacher said, "We want some boys to be pallbearers." There were muddy pools at the graveside. Their feet crunched on the gravel chips, and a teacher and a father or two and the hearse drivers kept close on each side as Robert and three other boys carried the coffin down 5A's row of honour, curling its toes in cold shoes. After the graveside service the hearse left, puffing a lot of exhaust smoke into the chilly air.

Robert began attending church after that, and at dinner one evening he announced that he had been asked to teach Sunday School. Auntie Alice smiled, but Mrs Saxby broke the peace. It made her quarrelsome whenever he said anything about church. She could not understand him. But Robert could not explain that he was always worried and thought about death all the time, about how it might come from behind the Iron Curtain, about Gypsy getting run over, about the girl next door dying, poof, just like that, and no one even knowing she was ill. He felt driven. "And besides," Mrs Saxby went on, "I thought you hated the idea of teaching." Robert adopted a stubborn look, a look like his father's, and taught at the Sunday School for a year or so. But when Ivan discovered him for the Drama Society in his second year at the university, he gratefully let religion slip away.

25

INCOMPLETE

In the first year he felt rootless. Dutifully he scribbled away in lectures, got his essays in on time, and sometimes he caught the bus back to the campus in the evenings to listen shyly to a debate from the back of a room or see a film. He joined the Labor Club because of Mrs Saxby, and played tennis for a university team. But he wanted someone to share things with. Geoffrey, who was studying medicine, was unapproachable.

Robert was surrounded by dedicated girls who talked seriously about the poems and novels they were studying, and took the initiative when it came to walking up into the city to see a film or go to a wine bar or a cafe for real coffee. They liked to talk about things. Some of them looked nettled with him afterwards. They seemed to say, "Well, what are your opinions about..." Everything about them told him he was a step behind. He was left with the poorer fellows in coats and ties, who were on Teaching Scholarships. They carried their notes about with them in briefcases and left him behind in tutorial discussions. It was said that the girls were there only for husbands. Robert seemed to be the only one doing the course with no purpose in mind. He wanted friends. He felt incomplete.

26
Ivan

Robert knew that he had another side to himself. It was discovered by Ivan and Nadine when he joined the Drama Society in his second year at the university. They were seductive, irreverent, interested in him for some reason. Ivan had come to the country when he was thirteen, just after the war. He had a dark, tossing manner. He wore high black leather boots or sandals and a sloppy black jumper. He talked about jazz and Brecht and knew all the older students. He made the Drama Society hum, challenged the lecturers, appeared to drop in and out of courses. He was like a troubador in the lives of the drama students.

Robert learned to drink vodka with Ivan, Ivan sprawled on a cushion next to him, talking about the plays he had seen, the interpretations he would one day make, the parts he had in mind for Robert to play. Rehearsals were scheduled, and Robert learned to sit on floors and idly be kissed by people and drink red wine with cheese and fists of bread. His first hangover cheered him, like a badge that he had earned. He swaggered a little.

At rehearsals Ivan would ask, "How come you're still living with your parents?" He thrust a book of obscure poetry into Robert's hands and said, "Read this." He cajoled and said, "I wouldn't be doing this if I didn't see something in you." There always seemed to be an undercurrent of fury in everything he said and did. Ivan hugged him, praised him, teased out his opinions and invited him home for dinners cooked by Nadine, the dark, combative girl who might or might not be his wife. Robert felt grateful and afraid and, to please Ivan, he made an effort to leave home and find a room in a house with other students.

27
LINGERING THINGS

A Taiwanese lecturer lived in the biggest room, disappearing inside it for days at a time and emerging to cook egg-flower soups or say goodbye to alarming young women who always seemed about to go horseriding or bushwalking. Robert listened to their awful ringing departures and never learned to understand a word that Peter Lim said. In the next biggest room lived a psychology student who yawned and belched and scratched his way into the bathroom and left behind him hair-cream on the others' combs, hairs trampled into the sodden bathmat and other lingering things. This man's brother lived there as well; he was a plump, tired public servant who had made an exotic den out of the rickety single-roomed bungalow in the backyard. Robert was ignored by the brothers, Peter Lim did not stop talking to him whenever he emerged from his bedroom, and someone regularly cheated on the food kitty.

Robert developed an interest in his clothes. He wished that he could dress like Ivan, but he lacked the courage. Instead he noticed that if he sponged at a stain on the knee of his gabardine trousers the ironed crease disappeared. He taught himself to sew on buttons and fasten a dragging cuff. He bought a signet ring. He learned to tie a Windsor knot. He bought a tweed coat and patched its elbows with leather, and sometimes he wore a matching tweed hat. "You look like a racecourse spiv," said Mrs Saxby when he went home one weekend.

A few weeks later Peter Lim let it be known that he was cooking a feast for Chinese New Year. "He wants you to ask somebody to come," grunted one of the brothers to Robert during the week. At dinner Ivan rolled his eyes because of the brothers, tucked expertly into the meal with chopsticks, and winked because Nadine was getting along famously with Peter, who kept bringing in steaming dishes, his glasses misty with pleasure. Robert sensed that Ivan and Nadine were sitting back watching him with smiles, almost like parents.

Afterwards, on the footpath outside the house, Ivan clapped his arm around Robert's shoulders. "Not quite what I had in mind for you," he said, releasing Robert and taking Nadine's hand. "But it's a start."

Robert went back inside the house, thinking about Ivan and Nadine who might or might not be married, wondering how he could lose his virginity, about how, when Ivan had first put the idea of moving away from home into his head, he had made himself feverish thinking about a *mixed* household, living with creative people, living with girls who let you into their rooms that had double beds, sat on the loo unconcernedly while you had a shower, chatted to you, taught you what they knew, and had love affairs with you without complications. And thinking about Nadine, who had knocked him backwards with kisses when she said goodbye just then.

28

A Meeting of Like Minds

Everything was new to Robert. He visited Ivan and Nadine two or three times a week, in the Holden sometimes if Mrs Saxby did not need it and he could be bothered to catch a tram or ride his bike round to pick it up.

Ivan and Nadine lived in an old weatherboard house that had paint peeling from the verandah posts. There was a constant smell of dampness rising from the smudged carpets and armchairs, hanging in their woollen jumpers. Ivan had a dog and Nadine had cats. Nadine curled on the floor on large cushions, watching, smiling slowly, a cat curled against her. Ivan, in his beret and black pullover, declaimed around the room, breaking off to exchange smirks with his setter.

At other times Robert liked to sit chatting with Nadine at her kitchen table, while Ivan burst in on them now and then to announce an innovation, his finger stabbing at a playscript, Nadine tolerantly looking away from Robert to discuss the changes and then turning back to him again. She wore loose, colourful clothes and let her straight black hair fall free of clips or fancy styles.

Robert liked to tell himself that love was a meeting of like minds, but he could not help feeling that his body and Nadine's, both of them narrow and coiled and quick, would fold together perfectly. He tried not to think about Ivan with her. Ivan, exposed and artless, and that black, curling beard. Nadine herself never spoke about Ivan, not with praise, love or dislike. Robert asked himself: does this mean she's free to love me?

And so he continued to cut meat into cubes for her or help her make sauces, while she analysed the Drama Society members, her family, her old lovers. She encouraged his own observations. They became sly and indulgent about everybody, and they each felt the security of Ivan in the next room growling into a tape recorder and prowling across and around the carpet, his stage.

29

INSTANT AMENDMENTS

When he was acting, Robert had a sense of watching something take shape and being able to make instant amendments to it. It must be like that for a painter, too, he thought. He said this to Ivan during one of their long pub sessions.

"It's more interesting to start things off and then see what happens," Ivan replied.

At that time everyone else wanted to perform plays

like *Look Back In Anger*, but Ivan decided to take ordinary situations and put them out of kilter. He marched Robert, Nadine and the other Drama Society members exultantly out of the pub, along the footpath, bundled them into a waiting tram, and lined them up on a bench opposite a man in a hat reading a newspaper. "Nothing could be more ordinary," Ivan whispered. As the tram shook and rattled out to a suburb, Robert could feel Nadine's arm and leg squeezed warmly against his side.

Craning forward to look at the man's newspaper, Ivan said, "The Prime Minister, Mr Menzies, said yesterday ..."

The newspaper crackled a little.

"Have a look at this," said Ivan, leaning closer. "Says here, 'A jockey was hurt when his mount stumbled after failing to take a jump in the Oaks Steeplechase yesterday'. And what about the poor bloody horse? No one gives a damn about the horse, he just gets a bullet in the head if he's injured and can't make any more money for the owner."

The man folded the newspaper and held it close to his face.

"The crossword," said Ivan with pleasure. He got onto his hands and knees on the floor and peered up at the underside of the newspaper. "Oh, damn, it's the cryptic. 'All in the pink, on side with your mother'." He turned around and looked at Robert and the others. "Any clues? Rob? Nadine?" Still on the floor, Ivan backed in against the man's knees to get a better look at the newspaper. "Let's see...pink gin, mother, mum, ma...*marginal*. Jesus."

He got up and sat alongside the man, whistling contentedly, tunelessly, and began to read over the man's shoulder. "Summit conference," he muttered. "The new leader of the Federal Opposition, Mr Calwell, today announced..." He looked across at them and said happily, "I met him once, did I ever tell you? When I was a refugee kid just off the boat. He came down the docks to welcome us." Ivan returned to the paper again. "Husband wife drown freak wave..."

"Do you mind?"

"Pardon?"

"Buy your own bloody paper."

The man opened his newspaper to its full extent, ballooning out its creases defiantly to erect a wall to block them out. Robert hugged himself with delight, but was afraid that Ivan might be reserving a role for him in all this. Nadine continued to sit close to him, giving warmth to his arm and leg, even though someone had left the bench to give these rowdies more room. Warily, with a tiny thrill of treachery in his gut, Robert watched Ivan rest his arms on his knees and incline his head to read something at the bottom.

"'The Decline of the Avant Garde'," he read. "What garbage. Says here what people want is a representation of real life. Well, today was made in heaven," and he pulled delicately at a corner of the paper to straighten it, patted his breast pocket, pulled out a pair of nail scissors with his other hand and busily snipped out the offending article. "Absolute garbage," he said, smoothing the cutting on his knee before folding it under his wrist-watch strap. The man sat utterly still, only his plump thighs trembling as the motor whirred at a tram stop.

30
A LOT TO RECLAIM

Ivan decided to take lunchtime plays to office workers. He rounded up the Drama Society members in order to whip up enthusiasm for his project and allocated little tasks to everybody. When Robert raised the problem of posters and handbills, Ivan clicked his fingers.

"Why don't we get your father to print them?" he said.

Robert was not so sure. For most of the time he had been able to keep his parents and his mild bohemianism separate from one another. Sometimes one threatened to spill over onto the other, so that he feared he did not seem genuine; for example, when he returned home for a weekend after not seeing Mr and Mrs Saxby for some time, he consciously had to moderate his Drama Society style — his frankness in conversation, his knowingness, his intensity — and when he joined Ivan and the others for coffee on Monday after such a weekend he felt almost gauche. He should have known better: he half understood that Mrs Saxby, her bosom flecked with cigarette ash, bringing out the wine and cheese for Bill Prior and the other members of the local branch of the Party, might have understood and welcomed his experiments at living but, subconsciously, he did not want to be identified with or embraced by anything to do with Bill Prior, and he did not want to make his father feel any more isolated than he already was.

"Why don't you ask him?" Ivan persisted. "Ask him how much he'll charge us for, say, a thousand handbills as well as a thousand programmes for each play."

Robert went home on Friday evening, sat down to chops and vegetables, and mumbled to his father.

Mr Saxby was expansive. "Of course, son. Tell your friend that will be no trouble at all. Tell him to drop round a mock-up and we'll work out the type you want, the colours, any pictures, whatever. It won't cost you much. Be pleased to do it." Both Mr and Mrs Saxby were looking at Robert with new eyes. "I'm glad you've got an interest in theatre, son."

At five o'clock on Monday Robert, wearing his overcoat thrown over his shoulders, swept into the Drama Society office and said, "My father said he'd do the printing for us, and he won't charge much."

"Good," said Ivan, reaching out his long fingers to spin around some papers on his desk. "These are some rough sketches I made. What do you think?"

To seal the deal, and because it was coming up to Robert's birthday as well, Ivan insisted on dinner in a restaurant. "You, me, Nadine and your parents. Do they like eating Italian?"

Mr and Mrs Saxby had accepted the idea of the Drama

Society, but Robert did not know if they would accept Ivan and Nadine. He felt beset.

"What's their number?" said Ivan.

"What?"

"Their phone number. I'll ring them now and fix it up."

On Friday night Mr and Mrs Saxby, dressed up and excited, picked Robert up in the Holden and they drove to Franca's in the city. "Don't be alarmed by them," said Robert from the back seat of the car. "They're a bit colourful, that's all." Mrs Saxby turned around and said, "Well, I think that's a recommendation. You mustn't start apologising for your friends before we've even met them. You must give us some credit. And naturally we're interested in the things you've been doing." Saying, "Sorry," Robert slumped back into his corner. "I'm looking forward to this," said Mr Saxby, parking the car.

Nadine and Ivan met them outside the restaurant. "Perfect timing," said Nadine. She kissed Robert and held out her hand to Mr and Mrs Saxby, smiling warmly, drawing Ivan in to meet them.

Robert was silent during dinner. He felt that he had a lot to make up for: he should not have imagined that Nadine and Ivan would dress or act freakishly, or talk to shock, or send up his parents. In fact they did not behave badly at all. He had been guilty of building up their differences, that was all. Nor should he have expected less of his parents. They all got on famously. Mrs Saxby and Nadine were profound, droll and salty, taking to one another like lovers, while Mr Saxby, perhaps hearing in Mrs Saxby's laugh an echo of her chats with bloody Bill Prior, ignored the two women and turned to Ivan. He shook his head at Ivan's tale of dislocation, as though he could see the little orphaned, cut-about boy scratching a living from scraps and thieving in the soot and bricks and ruins of his city in Europe. Robert could not hear what Nadine and his mother were saying to each other, but Nadine's thin brown wrists turned in the air, tumbling her bracelets, and her eyes in the shadows often caught the light. Mrs Saxby nodded and replied. He saw them touch each other's arms, and when it was time to go home they kissed.

In the car he said foolishly, "They're not married."

Mrs Saxby turned on him. "Does that matter? They're lovely, both of them. You're fortunate to have them as friends. Isn't Nadine beautiful? I haven't talked like that with anyone for ages. The girls I teach with are so young and silly in comparison, I've been starved for something different."

"That Ivan was an interesting bloke," said Mr Saxby.

31
CONTAINED

Ivan's troupe launched its series of plays with a special evening performance for family and friends. Nadine ushered Mr and Mrs Saxby to the best seats. They had begun to look upon Robert with new eyes and Mrs Saxby liked to say that she knew he was in good hands. Nadine, with her laugh, her beauty and her continental ways, was exactly the kind of wife she envisaged Robert having. In a thoughtful, teasing voice she said, "I wonder if she'll marry Ivan," giving Robert a keen look as though to see what his feelings were and to dare him to do something about it. She had lunch with Nadine sometimes. It seemed strange to Robert that they could become friends and he kept an anxious eye on them.

After the first night's performance there was a party, but Mr and Mrs Saxby did not stay, explaining that they would only be in the way. Which was just as well, thought Robert. Everyone got very drunk very quickly and drove to houses that he had not visited before. All the dark, dramatic girls in the Drama Society lived in terrace houses and had large beds, scatter cushions, jazz records and foreign books lying around. Silent men came in and out of rooms, sat down with the girls for a while, smoking, saying something clever and tired, and Robert recognised them as senior figures at the university, speakers at forums in the quadrangle.

Later everyone drove to Ivan's and Nadine's house. At about half-past one they all surged out again but Robert felt too tired to go with them. He sat propped against a wall by the record player, playing a soft jazz song over and over again. He had been helplessly sick behind a tree at the last house. He concentrated hard on the music, keeping his eyes steady, fighting down his illness. Nadine sat down with him. Stroking her cat, she spoke sadly about an unhappiness in Ivan: "The same old thing again." Robert could not concentrate. She lay on her back with her head in his lap and he tangled his fingers in her hair.

They started to dance and kiss, and Nadine undid the buttons on his shirt and Robert took off her jumper. In the bedroom they sprawled and kissed wetly for a while, Nadine's bra still fastened but its empty cups like dewlaps on the tops of her breasts. They fell asleep at some stage and at three o'clock Robert woke up and saw himself as a rake looking down at his sleeping conquest with profound tenderness, a tired cynical man who might never find innocent love again. But the mood evaporated because he felt cold and exposed, they had left the light on, he felt sticky but could not remember it happening, and Ivan might come home at any minute.

Nadine plunged out into the night with Robert to say goodbye. She was still drunk, bumping against door frames, infinitely yearning and sad as she kissed him.

He saw her at a barbecue the next day. With his hangover under the hot sun, terribly conscious of her sitting just across the lawn from him, Robert felt expansive with desire and knowledge, and at the same time was telling himself that nothing had *really* happened, at least, not that Nadine knew, since his own experience had been contained by layers of clothing. He gazed at her. She was defeated by the sun, her hangover and perhaps remorse as well, nursing her eyes under a large hat. Back to being a cat again.

32
NEED TO KNOW

The following Sunday afternoon Robert arrived at Nadine's with a bottle of wine and settled himself at her kitchen table. He was expectant: they would cook something expensive and elaborate, and she would say something. He chatted to her, waiting for her to remember. But she lifted groceries out of her shopping basket without comment and handed him knives for peeling and cutting. She turned to him with an effort whenever he spoke.

"Where's Ivan?" he said finally.

"Out."

They cooked and ate. The house was terribly quiet. "You know how he gets sometimes," she said. Robert did not: he felt that he knew nothing.

During the next few days he waited at home for her to ring, or rushed home from lectures to see if his housemates had scribbled a message on the pad next to the telephone. He wondered if, should someone like Mrs Saxby ask him, he could claim to be having an affair with Nadine.

For the next three weeks he evaded them, but that was no good, it was up to him, and so he borrowed the Holden and visited them. They opened the door to him, saying, with puzzled looks, "Where have you been lately?"

He could not work them out. He looked sharply at Ivan, but Ivan was unchanged, amiable, scornful and challenging as usual, and Nadine lay curled near him like a cat on the rug in front of the log fire. "Help yourself to some wine," she said, smiling lazily.

I'm too nice, thought Robert. Selfish people always

discover me. He boiled inside. Women like Nadine are always ripe for romanticising a bleakness of the soul of some arsehole bloke. The way she automatically assumes that Ivan's depression is of a special nature compared to everyone else's. The way she assumes the world has to stop and wait deferentially while she helps him through his little crisis. When probably all he needs is a good kick in the backside. Jesus.

Robert told himself, "I need to know." He stepped up his visits to see her, sitting with her and holding her leg between his own under the kitchen table. He bought her roses, watching for favour in her eyes. Her face grew worried. Robert's anxiety increased. Had she told Ivan anything? Ivan merely grinned and said things like, "Do you think your parents would mind if we had their car tonight to put up posters?" or "Do you think you could hand these out in the city?"

Robert composed a letter. He admitted his love in a way that was at once intense and indifferent, and he hinted darkly at things that might make her jealous but not drive her away. He wrote four drafts before he posted it, wondering if he was refining it too much, losing his spontaneity. He wondered if typing it had made it seem cooler and tougher.

He hoped that he was not making a nuisance of himself. Nadine seemed to be weary of the world, years wiser, a mixture of cross, kind and busy. "Oh Robert," she said. "Please don't like me too much."

33
STRUT AND RAGE

Soon Robert was feeling self-conscious about the Drama Society's activities and he sulkily refused to accept roles in any of the short plays that Ivan was taking to the city's office workers. He sat fuming in a tram while Ivan cut off the ends of people's cigarettes and smoked them, kindly holding a flaring match to the stub remaining in their bemused mouths. In their pub talks Robert suggested other ploys. He had just read about the panic caused when someone sent a telegram to several acquaintances saying *All is discovered. Flee at once.* "Or," he suggested, "We could send the wrong letter to people. For example, make a wife think her husband sent her a letter to his mistress by mistake."

Ivan looked at him. "You haven't been listening, have you?" he said. "You haven't seen what I mean when I cut up someone's newspaper or try five different sorts of hats on someone. Your ideas are only practical jokes, and they're cowardly because you're not putting yourself into the story you've set up."

Oh, bloody go to hell. Robert wanted to act in a proper role. He wanted to strut and rage in plays that were like living moments in someone's house somewhere. Last term they had put on *Look Back In Anger*: Robert had played Jimmy Porter and everyone had praised him. The last words of the review in the student paper said 'See it, if only for Robert Saxby's performance in the role of Jimmy Porter'. And now Ivan was saying he had no time for plays like that. "I want to innovate," was what he said now. Robert wanted to stand on a stage and hold an audience in the palm of his hand again.

Robert took the posters and handbills Ivan gave him and furtively left a few of them on shop counters and in hotel bars. He said that he was busy. He said that he had arranged to see a film, or that he had essays to write, exams to prepare for. He went to live at home again, taking the pile of yellowing Drama Society posters with him because he needed scrap paper, heaping them at the bottom of his wardrobe with shoes and clothes on top of them because he knew he could not meet Mrs Saxby's disapproving face if she found them. Somehow, it would be worse if she found out than if the others did.

And so, when Georgina said hello one day after the exams, he was on the lookout for love.

34

UNSTUDIED NATURE

He had been watching Georgina for some time from the back of lecture theatres and from the most comfortable chair under the window in the tutorial room. He had gazed at her, pale and unrequited, knowing that she was quite unlike Ivan and Nadine and the Drama Society types ("I don't really fit in with them," he rehearsed). Usually she was early, sitting alone and indifferent in the middle of the front row of seats in lecture theatres, so that he always looked there first when he entered these rooms, receiving once or twice a grudging flicker of a look in return for the face-splitting grins that he could never control. "Why don't you ask her out?" said Ivan, who sometimes came to lectures with him. "How long are you going to string the poor girl along with your winning smile?" Robert noticed that Georgina, like the others, appraised Ivan with long cool looks as they entered together, and an unbidden emotion told him that being in Ivan's company would raise Georgina's estimation of him. But he also crankily imagined Georgina sitting there with her blank face thinking about wrapping herself around Ivan in a rush of passion.

He was ready for love when she stopped outside the examination room and said, "Hello. Have you finished for the year too? Do you want to come and see a film this afternoon?" He let himself walk with her into the city to see a French film and, when she tapped her fingernail on his watch glass as they shared an observation about the film over coffee afterwards, the unstudied nature of it claimed him. Ivan and Nadine fled from his mind.

35
Tormented

Georgina offered enough, and kept enough back, to fill him with ardour and sentiment. They drove the Saxby Holden to distant beaches, and in the evenings they played tennis on the leafy court in the garden of her father's house. He was tormented by her legs.

He told her that he loved her. Her eyes closed and she cuddled against him in the front seat of the car. "Love *you*," she would say.

In one of their idle conversations Georgina told Robert that she loved the summer and hated the winter. He had not thought very much before about liking or disliking seasons but now, after considering it, he thought that he liked summer best too. They swam, played tennis and gazed with meaning at one another dressed in bathers. "All in good time," Georgina would say to him in the Holden, seated in her bathers on a wet towel folded double, taking her hand away from its brushing at the salty hair on his legs, the edge of her palm almost but never quite coming up far enough on his leg.

36
Indirect

They liked to sit for hours on her parents' couch, kissing. Courting Georgina taught Robert about being indirect. "Let's wait until we can have our clothes off," she might say, pushing him away. She meant, "Let's wait until we're married." Robert would then start his love-making all over again, sometimes taking an hour to reach the stage at which Georgina would make her interruption.

Tonight she pushed him away and went to the kitchen

to make coffee. She wheeled it in on the traymobile, frowning a little as the cups rattled. They both listened: sometimes her mother called sleepily from the bedroom down the hall, "Is that you, dear?"

Georgina poured the coffee and sat down beside Robert again. She kicked off her shoes and curled her legs beneath her. Robert rested his arm across her shoulders and she said "Mmm," and leaned against him. His hand was now within stroking distance of her breasts but he knew he would need up to half an hour before he could start dallying there. Instead, he gently traced her jaw, cheek, nose, lips and eyes with his fingertips. He knew that her ear was sensitive and so he was building up to that. His other hand was out at an awkward angle; he made a large adjustment of his body on the couch to get comfortable, whispering, "Sorry," into her ear.

Now he was free to do something with his other hand. He kissed the top of her head. She settled comfortably against him, giving a little sigh as he placed his arm around her waist to give her a friendly, brotherly pat on her stomach. Kissing was awkward because her head was now under his jaw. He concentrated on her head with his mouth for a while to distract her from what his hands might be about to do now that the fingers of one hand were hooked inside the waist band of her skirt, warming against her skin, and the fingers of the other hand were sliding along her collarbone and down a little each time he made a sweep. Still on this distraction business, Robert's shoeless toes and hers were engaged in flicking against one another.

He concentrated on her head, nuzzling into her hair. "Your hair smells nice." He kissed her crown, sliding his mouth down to brush against her ear so that she shivered. This was not a movement to hurry or rush into because if he put his tongue into her ear it might galvanise her, which invariably meant that she twisted upright and said, with infinite regret, "Darling, it's late," at which he would hold her head in both his hands while he looked into her eyes for a heartfelt moment and then lean forwards to give her a tender kiss on the forehead, wanting to scream his fucking head off.

Avoiding this possibility, Robert kept up the nuzzling of her head and a circumscribed smoothing of her skirt over her stomach and hip joints. He thought that they both were thankful to put off actual kissing for the moment. Before the coffee break they had had an epic kiss that involved quite a lot of dribbling and furtive wipes — I hope it's not *my* mouth producing all that — teeth clicking together because she had once said she found that exciting, little bites, swollen lips and eventual weariness with the whole business.

Nestling even closer to him, Georgina arched her head back and pursed her lips, as though abandoning herself to his hand which was now well and truly under her blouse, so that his knuckles were touching the stiff underside of her bra but not quite brushing the underside of her breasts. Robert knew that the angle was bad because his head was uppermost and dribble flows downhill every time. He concentrated on not producing spittle or repaying the warm gust of coffee breath that greeted him, while at the same time stepping up the description his fingers were making of her hips. Minutes later, a final, frank gesture, and immediately she went slack. "My darling," she said, sighing and giving him a jolly slap on the knee, "It's late and I've got an early lecture tomorrow morning."

Even so his actual departure was delayed. First the cups had to be rinsed, there was a certain amount of giggling on the doorstep, she broke away suddenly and said, "Alexander! I haven't fed Alexander," and he followed her back to the kitchen while she spooned something into Alexander's bowl. Then back to the door again, the food bowl placed on the cement path next to Mrs Allynson's geraniums in pots, then finally she gave him the kiss goodbye and the little sigh of foreverness (keeping her hips well clear); and Robert's last glimpse of her, until the next time, was a big smile before she brought the cat up to her chin and rocked to and fro. "Mmmm, bye bye."

37
His True Nature

"Jeanette's taken you out of yourself, son," said Mr Saxby one day as they discussed the team for the Third Test match. "Georgina, Dad," said Robert. "Her name's Georgina."

Mrs Saxby always said a short, "Hello Georgina," and then left the room whenever Georgina visited the Saxby home. She would say, as she paused in the doorway, "If you like, tell Georgina she can stay for dinner with us, Robert." (Bloody wouldn't hurt you to ask her yourself, would it?) Mr Saxby would turn around in his kitchen chair and watch his wife depart, and then say apologetically to Georgina, "She's very busy these days, what with the election coming up." Georgina often hissed in Robert's ear when she was alone with him, "Does your mother like me? She doesn't, does she?"

"I'm sure she does," he said.

But it seemed expedient to avoid his house. Georgina's parents were livelier anyhow, sweeping through the hot summer days on a tide of picnics, beach outings, tennis and cold, highly alcoholic drinks. He thought of Nadine only once, and shook his head at how unsuitable she had been for him and how ignorant she must have found him. Nadine was too quick and dark and clever and selfish, a combination that kept him on edge and was no good for him. Georgina was suntanned, peaceful and beautiful in a sleepy kind of way. Much more suitable. He wanted to say to his mother that she could not see the Georgina that he saw. Obviously he could not tell her about Georgina in bathers touching his leg, or Georgina saying things like, "It would be lovely to stay a night with you." Robert suspected that his mother wanted him to meet someone like Nadine. Perhaps she had given up on Mr Saxby but thought that her son could still be an interesting man, and that Georgina was not going to be much help. Perhaps she looked at Georgina's peaceful face, lovely clothes and interested, obliging manner, and thought her silly and empty. "Nadine is such a lovely girl," she said from time to time. So what that Nadine was lovely? Things happen when people are thrown together day in and day out, and his mother should have been able to accept that things were not always going to stay the same, and therefore she shouldn't have muttered darkly about his true nature and likely future when she heard that he had left the Drama Society and was seeing Georgina every day. "She's very sweet," said Mrs Saxby after Georgina had been to lunch one day. "Very neat and well-mannered."

Well, bugger her. How would she know what it had been like for him when, at a stage in his life where one day had been pretty much like another, Georgina had come into his life one afternoon and tapped on the glass of his wrist-watch with her long, vibrating fingernail.

38

WHAT A MONSTER

One day Georgina announced that she wanted to buy a car. Robert offered to help and over the next two weeks, on Thursday afternoons and all day on Saturdays, they visited second-hand car yards and depressing houses tucked away in suburbs he had never heard of. "Nope," Georgina would say, and they would drive on.

Mr and Mrs Saxby let him borrow the white Holden for these trips. Here and there metal showed through the paint, and the car now had a distinct lean on its left side. It had done 150 000 miles, "And doesn't look like stopping," said his father. "Your mother's taken bloody good care of that car." Horsehair fibres stuck out of the upholstery and they had to find something for Georgina to sit on before they could get under way.

And so they looked at seventeen private cars and nine dealers' cars, the Holden lurching with an alarming heave around corners and racketing up hills. "Not much demand for these any more, mate," said the dealers. "Pardon? *Not* selling. You're after a car for the young lady here. Right, right, right." Georgina, lips pursed, gay from the attention, jumped into and out of every car and at the end of the day would wail, "I want something a bit *different*. I know this one's reliable, I know this one's cheap, but I don't want it. I want something a bit different."

One day they met a dealer, a big man with plump hands like dough that he kept tucked away under his arms or in his pockets. "A bit different," he said. "Now let me see...There's the wife's car, a Riley. Only come in last week, and she's been using it as a runabout till I can get her something else. Want to have a look at it?"

The dealer settled into the back seat of the Holden and gave Robert directions to his house. His wife looked up tiredly at them from a flower bed. "She's been a bit down this past week," he said, "so she uses the car to get out and about." His wife backed the car out of the garage for them and stood a long way back. "British racing green," he said, patting the elegant bonnet. "Classy, go forever, not a trace of smoke. Take it around the block and I'll get the wife to make some tea."

In the sitting room he named a price and said, "I'll just go out in the kitchen and give the wife a hand with the tea things while you think it over." He lowered his voice and leaned over them. "Sorry about the wife: she had a bit of a setback last week — our boy ran out in the road and got run over by a van. So," he said, straightening up, "think it over. Cost you more if I'd done it up and put it in the yard, of course."

Robert and Georgina sat in the cold room. Georgina

leaned against him and whispered, "Can you lend me £20? I really like it but I haven't got quite enough for the deposit." The man and his wife came back. The woman sat by the door and held out her cup while her husband gently poured tea into it, saying, "All right, love?" He turned to them and said, "Tell you what — I'll chuck in a free service and my mechanic'll give her the once over, and you can have her late tomorrow."

Georgina was excited on the way home. She made jokes about the Holden. She hoped the dealer would get his wife another car soon. "Gee, what a monster," she said.

To celebrate, Georgina took Robert for a long drive down the coast the next weekend. He showed her the hotel where the Saxbys stayed when he was younger, and a few miles farther on Georgina stopped the Riley so that they could stand on a cliff-top and look into a small cove. She pointed to the far side, at a promontory that looked like a head butting into the ocean beyond it, and said, "That's The Point." She clasped Robert's arm. "I'd love to have a holiday house down here, wouldn't you?"

The Point was to become their favourite spot, Robert adopting it without demur. Clearly the Allynsons had had better, more adventurous holidays than the Saxbys in the past: there was not much that he could say about some old hotel and building sandcastles. Swinging their hands together, their eyes gleaming, they obliquely talked about what kind of house it would be and what they would do there.

39

A Part of It

Mr Allynson wanted nothing but the best for his girl, and her twenty-first birthday party was going to be a slap-up do. Robert and Georgina worked out a guest list.

"I think it's sad you don't see Ivan and Nadine any

more," she said. She handed him another envelope to address. "I want at least some of your friends to come."

Robert was very conscious that, for the past year, he had not been friendly with anyone apart from Georgina and her friends — some of whom he did not like. He supposed that if he asked Nadine and Ivan then he could ask one or two others from his Drama Society days, and there were three blokes from his school days who had entered university with him. Really, he did not want to ask anyone. Ivan and Nadine would wear their mocking eyes, make oblique references to him running away or letting them down, and they would be cynical about Georgina — think him shallow, his head turned by her clothes, the Allynson house, her sense of the proper way to do things. "They'll add a splash of colour to the proceedings," she said, writing carefully on another card with her violet ink.

Mr and Mrs Allynson provided the drink, the food and the house. "The rest is up to you young ones," said Laurie Allynson expansively. "If you want us we'll be down the other end of the house where we can't bother you."

The enormous Allynson rooms were ideal for a party. One hundred invitations requesting "and friend" were sent out and most people said they would love to come, and did. At nine o'clock Mr Allynson held up his hand, toasted Georgina with a catch in his throat, and left saying, "We'll leave you to it."

Robert thought that he should do a little judicious marshalling of the guests from time to time, later in the evening. During his rounds he came upon lovers trying a door handle, a girl he had not seen before standing desolate in the shadows, a heartsick boy on the verandah looking out at a couple sitting on a garden seat in the moonlight. Tactfully, benevolently, Robert slipped past them, keeping watch on the big, festive house, returning always to the brightness and noise and Georgina's claiming arm and smile; and, half-an-hour, an hour later, he eased away again for another tour, going wherever he liked by right: that's the fellow Georgina's going steady with.

Now and then he had to hurry down the polished floor of the long hall on tip-toe, whispering urgently to a lost, misdirected back: "Excuse me. Excuse me, sorry, that's private in there." At about midnight the light was still shining under the door at the back of the house. He knocked and looked inside. "Still up? Not keeping you awake, are we?" Mr and Mrs Allynson did not hear him at first. They were sitting listening to separate radios in armchairs far apart, books in their laps, a traymobile with cups of cold, grey coffee to one side, a pall of dissatisfaction hovering between the Sports Round-up and Music to Midnight. "Sorry," said Robert. "Didn't mean to disturb you." The Allynsons jumped to their feet. "Not at all, dear. Are you having a lovely time?"

Robert talked to them for a while and then returned to the party, loving the way Georgina drew him in to her side. She was talking to Ivan and Nadine, who greeted him with hugs and looked about them eagerly. "So this is where you've got to," said Nadine. "We've missed you." Robert felt his voice grow quieter, so that they had to lean to hear him, and his elbow was jostled, causing him to spill his drink. A year ago he had sent Nadine that foolish letter, and surely Ivan knew about it, and he suddenly thought of his silly walks through the house tonight and hoped that Nadine and Ivan had not seen him. He had an uncomfortable sense of their exacting standards, of his testing days with them, of his drifting away to something easier. He examined them anxiously and felt worse. They looked smaller than he remembered, but perhaps that was because they were in the middle of a crowd, and they were several years older than anyone else, with tired eyes and wrinkles that he had not noticed before. They were dressed in bright cottons, scarves and leather sandals but still looked diminished, somehow warm and assailable, amongst the shoving bodies in the Allynson lounge-room. Robert looked at the young, inelegant crowd and hoped that he did not look too much a part of it.

40
Mum and Dad

At the beach one afternoon, Robert and Georgina decided that they would announce their engagement on Christmas Day. "I think my parents were disappointed we didn't say anything at my party," said Georgina, "but I hate too much fuss." They agreed that Georgina would drive over in her Riley for the traditional Christmas lunch with the Saxbys and take Robert back with her to Mr and Mrs Allynson's in the afternoon. Georgina said that she did not want the two families to get together that day. "I don't think I could stand it," she said. Robert said all right but, as he was leaning on his elbow in the sand, tracing patterns around her brown, outstretched arm, he felt a rush of sentiment. He wanted Georgina to like his parents more than she did.

During lunch on Christmas Day, Mr Saxby blinked with emotion and toasted them. Mrs Saxby tended to be sardonic during the roast, but mostly she gazed at both of them with such an open face that Robert told himself she had simply been making jokes to cover her nervousness. She smoked her cigarettes and smiled. Georgina did not say very much.

"There's that old double bed you can have," said Mrs Saxby suddenly, her eyes bright, addressing Georgina.

"Now, now, mother," said Mr Saxby. "You're only embarrassing these young people."

They opened presents and spent a desultory afternoon in the sitting-room. Mrs Saxby, alert in her chair, was watchful, pouncing forward to fill Georgina's glass or offer her the plate of rum-balls at the slightest sign of any restlessness. "Have another drink, dear," she said, reaching with the bottle. "It's not every day we have an engagement." At four o'clock, at a sign from Georgina, Robert began an elaborate preparation for departure, looking at his watch and turning to Georgina and saying, "Hadn't we better...?" and saying loudly something silly about a year from now.

The Allynsons' style was quite different. They always had more and different sorts of things to drink, celebrated with a flourish, brought out the traymobile and served interesting food. Mr Allynson was noisy and Mrs Allynson said she sometimes went naked on hot days and had to go and put some clothes on when she heard Robert pulling up outside in the old Holden.

He made the announcement: he darted worried looks at Georgina's sly face, for she had been saying for weeks that he had to ask her father's permission first, and he had almost come to believe her. Mrs Allynson lifted her hands, dropped them in her lap, and sat back in her chair. "Oh," she said. "My lovely, lovely boy," and she kissed him. She turned to Georgina and kissed her. "My beautiful big girl," she said. "I knew it," shouted Mr Allynson. "Didn't I tell you they'd say something soon?"

Mr Allynson brought out a bottle of champagne. He stopped in the act of pouring it. "But what about Pat and Hartley?" he said. "Give them a ring, son. They should be here too."

"They send their love, Mr Allynson, and would love to celebrate some time or other," said Robert, "but they had to go out somewhere else."

He sensed Georgina relax in her chair. He felt that he was starting to know her.

"Oh Rob, you make us sound so old," said Georgina's mother. "I think it's time you started calling us something less formal."

"Call us Mum and Dad, son," said Georgina's father.

Robert gave Georgina her ring for the second time that day, and separately a large beach towel and an expensive bottle of scent. She gave him a gold letter-opener. His fingers lingered on it.

They ate cold turkey and salad, the tomatoes doused in vinegar. Robert found three sixpences in his pudding;

Mrs Allynson smiled fondly at him and then, overcome, reached across the table and clasped his hand. She darted away and came back with a spray can. "That blarmy blowie," she said. "Where did he go?" She peered down at the table. "I saw him nearly land on the pudding." Pumping the handle she tracked the blowfly through the room, spraying into dark corners and above their heads. A smell descended.

They finished with tea served in the Royal Doulton service in the sitting-room. Georgina's father took four spoonsful of sugar in his pale red tea. He was full of the news. He stirred his tea forty times, stopped, tapped his spoon on the edge of the cup, and then started all over again, full of plans for them.

Later Mr Allynson took Robert for a walk through the house, almost, thought Robert, as though he were about to present it as a gift. His future father-in-law was intimate and drunk and kept stopping in surprise in every room. Robert stood next to him in the big, dark rooms and waited. Mr Allynson had a pocketful of keys, and every now and then he unlocked a cupboard or a room or a drawer, looked around and locked up again. Robert realised that the house was shut up tight, and every key labelled, and every bottle, plate and scrap of private paper locked away somewhere. Mr Allynson, suddenly insecure and agitating his keys in his pocket, led him back to the sitting-room and fell asleep in an armchair.

41

THE KIDS

When they got married a year later, Robert inherited the Holden and they became a two-car family. They spent their honeymoon in a fabled hotel on a ferny ridge of a mountain range. Men approached them and asked if they were interested in selling the Riley, or told Georgina to enter it in a *concours d'élégance*. After their honeymoon, Robert and Georgina moved into a house owned by Georgina's parents and Robert met the headmaster of his first school and thought about lesson plans. They were gravely getting ready for Robert to be a husband who came home from work. Before he set off in the Holden for his first day at his first job Georgina kissed him goodbye at the front door. Mr and Mrs Allynson and Mr Saxby still referred to them as "the kids", but they were not kids any more.

42
DO BETTER

In the peaceful moments after instruction or discussion, Robert liked to sit and watch his pupils writing their essays or making notes from books he had got for them from the school library. They leaned over their books, writing or reading, or gazing in concentration or tiredness out of the window. They were good kids, gearing up for university next year. Robert had wide-ranging talks with them. They had clamorous intellects, were starting to use their heads. He wondered what the day-dreamers were thinking about. Sometimes he saw their eyes widen suddenly, or they showed tiny shocks or movements, or seemed to grow aware of something private.

One morning Robert grew aware of a face staring into the room from the corridor. He looked up. It was the headmaster, a man rarely seen unless he took over classes for teachers who were ill. The headmaster did not know the names of any of the pupils. He was a man who wore an academic gown and was filled with loathing and menace. "Do you know what he used to do?" said a friend over coffee in the Staff Room. "He would set the poor kids masses of work and just sit watching them, giving them the shivers. Then he would take the work home with a class photo and mark the work according to how he felt about the poor kids' faces. The things he wrote on their work, boy."

A girl looked around, discomforted. Robert coughed and stood up. Everyone stopped working and one or two of them began to respond to him as he tossed them ideas for the end-of-year play. He wrote things on the blackboard and the room buzzed with work. He wondered what kind of education he was giving these children and if he was very good at it. The headmaster's face disappeared.

Georgina told him he could do better. "You'll get stuck there," she said. The world was changing around them and her impatience was catching. She worked as an editor on a magazine and had brought some style into their lives. They were thinking of buying a house, especially now that Rosemary, their daughter, had been born. Like the youngsters that Robert taught, he and Georgina were touched by the music that was being played, and the lengths that people wore their hair and hems these days. Things were speeding up around them; the government was spending money. Georgina showed Robert the employment pages on Saturday mornings and impressed him with her faith in him, the satisfaction he would have, his better-than-even chance of getting one of those jobs. He had a good degree, had teaching experience, and there could not be too many experts around in film and drama studies. He would be getting in at the start of that new university that was all set to challenge the older, stuffier universities. She said they would be crying out for new people. She drew comparisons, asking him to consider so and so, a friend at work, or the husband of one of her friends: "He doesn't have much going for him, does he?" she said. "Yet look where he is." Robert liked being taken in hand, liked her confidence in him. He got the job: practically walked into it.

43
THE DEPARTMENT

When Robert joined the Department, Maggie Thiele took him under her wing. She had joined the Department two years earlier, in its infancy, and was now seen as an old hand by everyone. She came to be the one whom the staff sought for advice and information about the Department's workings, but it was they who charged up the promotion ladder while she, smarter and better qualified, remained on a solid rung somewhere underneath them. She told all this to Robert one day.

In March of the year that Robert joined the Department, Maggie held a Sunday luncheon at her house so that new staff members could meet everyone. Robert arrived late and stood uncertainly on the lawn at the back of the house, until Maggie came up to him and took him by the arm and drew him into the groups of people talking and drinking around tables under the fruit trees. Brian, her husband, showed him to the drinks table and told him to help himself. Robert took up a glasss of claret and eased away because he had just seen Gower approaching. A small, anxious man in walk socks that had slipped down, Gower, everyone knew, was in a bad way. It was said that his marriage was on the rocks, he had been told to stop smoking, and the book that he had been working on had been rejected by too many publishers. He was a man made fuzzy around the edges by drinking.

It was hot in the sun and so Robert stood under the leafiest tree, next to a child's swing. From this position he watched and waited until his bones felt loose enough for him to walk across the lawn and let himself be taken in by a circle of people. Maggie and Brian waved to him from time to time.

It was curious seeing them together. Maggie was open and always ready to laugh, and one of the first things she had said to Robert was, "Would you like a hit of tennis sometime?" Her husband Brian was the kind of man who hides his face from enquiry. He wore dark glasses outside the house, and a cigarette in his mouth. His hair fell over his temples and forehead, and his whiskers rushed down in sculptured slashes on each side of his face. There were two rings on the hand that held his jaw thoughtfully and a chain in the hairs at his throat.

Maggie and Brian did not let each other move out of sight. Robert joined a group by the table and watched them circle the lawn and trees and swings, listening to their guests, filling glasses, tending to the chops or flies on the salad, cheerful, loud and witty, finishing sentences for some duffer and each other too, a perfect conspiracy of thoughts and outlook.

"By saying it's not a civil war..." said Brian,

"...they can argue that it's our duty to help because an independent country is trying to resist outside aggressors," said Maggie.

Brian worked for the national broadcasting commission and his programme was irritating to the government these days, asking its representatives tricky questions, using newly discovered experts to explain how shoddy was the government's foreign policy, how attenuated its conscience and its knowledge of other cultures. The Department and its wives thrilled to Brian in a corner of the garden, the knowledgeable among them explaining things to him. Robert thought Georgina would regret staying at home with the baby.

The afternoon passed, and there were other such parties and dinners over the years: at election time, to say goodbye to someone who had floated free from the top of the ladder, to celebrate the publication of so and so's book, and now that the exams are over why not? Robert and Maggie became friends, Brian joining them for drinks or tennis as often as not.

In the early days Robert took Georgina to the parties and dinners. He discovered that she disliked Maggie and

Brian, that it was instant, reasoned and permanent. "You go ahead," she said. "I don't mind if you're friends with Maggie — in fact I'm glad you are. But she and I don't get on. And as for Brian."

44
Low, New and Stark

Robert quite liked their house. The garden had a wild scent from the flowering shrubs that needed cutting back, and the hallway was long, cool and dark, reminding him of the Saxby home. But when Rosie was two years old Georgina announced that she did not intend to live in the house another minute. She hated its coldness and gloom. She wanted something low, new and stark. The magazine was giving her plenty of work to do from home so that she could keep an eye on Rosie (with the help of Mrs Allynson from time to time) and, she said, with Robert's income coming in as well they certainly could afford something better. Perhaps at the end of the term they'd start to look, Robert suggested, but he came home one afternoon to find her triumphant. She bundled him into the Riley and took him to a suburb of slopes and broad streets lined with trees. There were no fences, only barriers of irreproachable lawns. She took him to a long white house built in two levels on the sloping land. "We can afford it," she said. A tiny plaque on the wall gave the architect's name and there was the number 18 in brass by the door. They came to call it "Degraves Street" and Georgina proceeded to fill it with bright modern things.

45
Discards

Robert invited his brother and sister to visit them in their new house. Geoffrey said that he was busy. Eleanor couldn't wait.

At one point during the afternoon, Robert found himself joining Georgina and Eleanor in the bedroom, where they were admiring Georgina's clothes. "Oh, that's beautiful," Eleanor was saying. "It looks so lovely on you."

She was sitting on a chair, curled up as though to comfort herself. Her eye was black where her husband had punched her and she had modest, high little pointy breasts under her twin-set. She gave a trembly smile as Georgina's discards mounted in her lap.

Robert sat on the side of the bed. Fervour glistened in Georgina's eyes. She pulled her glorious dresses from their hangers, held them against her body, strode across the room, flattened her stomach before the vanity table, and held her soft, costly underwear briefly against her cheek. Her words tumbled out with pleasure. She stripped something off and put on something else and spun around, overwhelming them.

Georgina always knew exactly what to wear and exactly what to buy for other people to wear. When she first met Auntie Alice she had recognised the old lady's inclination to give outsized, heavy, outmoded clothes to the family. "I never let anyone buy my clothes for me, Auntie Alice," she had said distinctly at their wedding reception, leaning across the trestle table. "I have a dress-maker, or there's a particular shop I go to." Auntie Alice had subsided a little in her chair. In December she had given them place mats.

The first time Robert bought Georgina some flimsy knickers and a bra, she dropped them back onto the tissue paper on the bed and said, "Darling, I wish you wouldn't buy me clothes. I'm too fussy, so it's best if I buy my own." She gave him a brief hug and said, "Oh, I'm sorry, it was such a lovely thought, too. What else did you buy today?" He modelled it for her. "I needed a new jacket," he said. "Blazer," she said, pinching at its shoulders critically. "It's a blazer."

46
HOUSE WARMING

Late in November Georgina and Robert invited some friends and colleagues to a buffet-style house-warming party to celebrate their purchase of Degraves Street. Georgina wanted everything to go smoothly and grew snappy and anxious with Robert, saying he wasn't making enough effort. But Robert found the new house to be too stern; he missed the clutter of the past and felt that he had to apologise to friends when they walked wide-eyed into it for the first time. He had suggested that his sister would love to help, that a party and helping Georgina cater for it would brighten Eleanor up a bit. He rang her and then he set off in Georgina's Riley to buy the drinks and odds and ends. He arrived back to find Eleanor and Georgina slicing, beating and quick-frying small balls of things. Eleanor looked much the same as usual, rather blurred and tired, her smile a little shaky. He walked into the room where they would hold the party, set up a table of drinks and practised making martinis. "Mmm, perfect," said Georgina, materialising to sip from his glass. Robert looked at the green-faced Eurasian woman in the print on the wall above the drinks table and quickly away again.

    He had invited three friends and their husbands from his old school-teaching days, as well as Eleanor and her husband, and Maggie and Brian Thiele. Robert also thought that he had better invite Gower and his wife, since Gower was going to be giving one or two lectures for him next year. Unfortunately Gower was the kind of man who embraces occasions too eagerly. But at least Maggie was coming. Robert was starting to think of her as his friend.

    Georgina invited Mr and Mrs Saxby and her own parents for drinks at six o'clock, and had hunted the four of them out the door again, Rosie in Mrs Allynson's arms, by half-past seven. Eleanor went home to change and fetch her husband, and the house was suddenly quiet. "They'll start arriving soon," said Robert from his armchair, watching Georgina's dissatisfied face eye the room.

By eight o'clock several sparkling women from her magazine had arrived, laughing and appreciative on their way into the house, suddenly stopping to appraise Robert. Their husbands, indifferent to the house, followed them, holding bottles aloft and signalling enquiries across the room to him. He stepped out from the dining table. "Here, let me take those," he said. Then his own guests arrived. Everyone had dressed up and the room was soon crowded.

The party proceeded successfully without much effort on anyone's part. They ate hungrily, were clever and cheerful in conversation with one another. Eleanor and Colin did not come; Robert hoped they were not fighting but he could imagine Colin's hectoring voice punishing Eleanor for having other loyalties, his mean, frightened punches to her head.

Robert could see Georgina's uncertainty when her editor suggested dancing. She had not intended that, was unprepared for it and looked quickly round to see if the room was suitable for dancing. He felt sorry for her. This party meant a lot to her and she hated anything unexpected, needing guidance in the right way of doing things. "But we haven't got any records to dance to," she said unhappily. "We have!" shouted the editor. We thought we'd bring some records along." The men groaned: "Old Judy's off again," but Robert saw that they were just as eager as their wives.

They danced the twist or faced each other in lines, reproducing each other's jerky mannequin gestures, or stomped shouting, "Love, love me DO! You know I love YOU!" They've got it all worked out pat, thought Robert. He sat watching the dancing, half listening to Gower, who was drunk and sarcastic and seemed afraid that someone might make him get up and dance. Maggie drifted up to them saying, "No piking allowed. Everyone up!"

"Clear off," said Gower.

"Charming," she replied, holding her hand out to Robert. "Come on, my sweet, don't waste your time with him."

Robert got up to dance, feeling hesitant and silly. After a while someone got out a comb and combed his hair down over his forehead like the kids were wearing it these days. Robert tried to catch Georgina's eye but she wore an expression of ghastly enjoyment and the constant changing of partners confused him. Somehow Maggie was dancing with someone else.

When they played some romantic music Robert thought that he would like to dance slowly and dreamily with Georgina, rest against her in the manner of the other couples, but she had disappeared. He found her sitting in another room talking eagerly to someone about an issue involving the magazine. "In a little while, darling," she said. "I have to finish talking over some work things with Alan." Robert sat down with them, idly listening until Georgina broke off and said, "Don't wait, darling. Perhaps you could see if everyone has a drink?" The man with her had an air of waiting and watching. He waited, with a half smile, for Robert to leave.

Robert went into the garden and smoked a cigarette. He could see Gower attempting to dance with his wife on the patio. Mrs Gower held her arms pressed tight to her sides and her face was expressionless, enduring her husband's face in her neck and his hands on her buttocks.

As everyone left, Georgina walked with them out to their cars to say goodnight. Robert started cleaning up. With a pencil he drew a thin moustache on the green-faced woman. Which was not so bad since Georgina had earlier announced that she was getting rid of it. No one had that painting hanging in their homes any more.

47
INSTINCT

It seemed like no time at all had gone by, and yet Rosie was starting school and Leigh had begun to totter around the house. Robert thought that it was a wonder there was not more incest in families. There were all those bodies growing, breathing, changing colour with the seasons, claiming equal rights over every nook and cranny in the house, releasing smells and functioning without explanation or apology, all within a small space.

Rosie liked to shower with him, gazing up at his penis and flicking it with a wash cloth. "Just don't do anything to scare her," said Georgina, observing this one day when she came into the bathroom. She herself told him that when Leigh came into bed with them in the mornings he liked to lie on top of her with his little erection and sleepily rub against her, his thumb in his mouth. "It's instinct, isn't it?" she said. "It must be." Rosie liked to sit astride Robert's chest and wrestle with him. He would wrap his arms around his daughter in growly tussles, overcome with love, clutched by her rubbery little legs, feeling himself stir a little. But it did not do to let Rosie's face get too close — her breath in the mornings was awful.

48
LIKE WATCHING HIMSELF

When each of his grandchildren was born, Mr Saxby seemed renewed. His breast and his smile expanded. Leigh, especially, was his favourite. Mr Saxby clowned and horsed around, fatuous and certain that life was good. Here was something that the Bill Priors of this world could not touch. He liked to swing Leigh into the air and catch him, throw balls to him, take him for walks in the park opposite the house. But Robert had to leave the room and block his ears, because watching his father whoop and play was almost like watching himself.

One day when Mr Saxby gave Leigh a glass of beer, tickled pink to see the little tacker smack his lips, Georgina angrily snatched back her son and said to Robert and Mr Saxby, "He's not a sideshow attraction."

She was the better parent, Robert thought. She did not fuss or treat the children unfairly; she merely seemed tired of them sometimes. She was practical and generous with her love. She did not twist inside with remorse at what they, as parents, had done wrong or failed to do. She was comfortable and peaceful with them, bundling them into her lap, singing songs with them, grooming their ears and faces with her lips and fingernails.

And yet she was fastidious about everything else, her nose always ready to wrinkle in distaste or disapproval, her body and clothes always clean and pressed. When she abandoned herself to the children's bodies, and on those nights when she had a rude enjoyment of Robert in bed, she might never have had a nose that lifted away from things. She kept Robert on his toes. Often he was surprised by the strength of her feelings and the feelings he didn't know about. She sat on the couch with her arms around the children one evening after a futile argument with him, rubbing her jaw on the tops of their shampooed heads, unexpected tears in her eyes as she avoided looking at him. "You two are my best friends," she told the children. She put her hands deep into the pockets of their dressing gowns. "You're the only ones I can trust."

49

Ascendancy

One day Georgina caught herself feeling incongruous, said, "We need a larger car for the children," and sold the Riley. Rosemary was seven and Leigh four and, with all the paraphernalia of toys, nappies, the cot, medical things and clothes, there no longer was enough room in the Riley. The old Holden was unreliable, she pointed out, and what with his job and her job they could afford a new car. One Friday Robert came home to find a new white Ford Galaxie with white-wall tyres parked outside Degraves Street. The next day Georgina drove them into the hills for Devonshire Tea.

Later the Galaxie swept them without effort down the highways of the land to summer holidays in other states. The large back seat seemed to swallow up the children, keeping them cosy and docile, their little legs dangling. In the boot were buckets and spades and cases, the white-walled tyres got tarry, the motor rumbled in a satisfying way when they slowed to turn off the road for petrol, and in that car Georgina and Robert could pass any vehicle in their path.

The Galaxie stood out in the forecourts of the petrol stations or hotels at which they stopped, and Robert, checking the unchanging oil and water levels in the early morning before the next stage of their journey, covertly observed by other hotel guests who were pouring water into their radiators, found that he was learning something about the sense of ascendancy that Georgina gained from excellent and expensive things. He would nod hello to the other hotel guests. His Italian leather shoes made clean, fulfilling sounds as he circled the car.

50

DECISIONS

In the past Robert had always spent his money in an idle fashion, never over-reaching himself, simply spending what he had and no more. It was Georgina who introduced him to saving. With her income as well as his own, they were able to afford to pay off Degraves Street, go on holidays, have nice things.

Georgina made the decisions about their money and

priorities. She had held out until the market was at its lowest before buying Degraves Street, she had put the children's names down for schools that were almost in the top bracket, and she put their savings into separate accounts for day-to-day expenses, holidays and buying fine things from time to time. She was generous at Christmas time and birthdays, and argued that Rosie and Leigh should be given more than enough pocket-money so that they need not feel frustrated or act in a mean way. Robert did not like to say anything about her personal account — he did not mind that she had one, but she did keep the account book hidden, never ever mentioned it. There was a dark air of secrecy about the whole thing, and he could imagine Mrs Allynson saying to Georgina before they married, "Always keep a little tucked away, dear."

And then Georgina inherited ten thousand dollars from her grandmother and reminded Robert of their promise to one another. It had to be The Point, she said. They could not conceive of having a holiday house or future summers anywhere else. Land prices were still low and Mr Allynson told them he had contacts who could build them a house very cheaply.

Soon things were running like clockwork. Georgina reviewed their situation regularly, choosing a Sunday morning every month to sit at her desk with bills, paper clips, fountain pen, cheques and stamped envelopes scattered around her and a blue- and red-lined ledger book before her. She usually finished this task by lunchtime and came into the lounge-room bright-eyed with accomplishment: she had said a long time ago that she would never be like her mother, whom her father had not ever allowed to write a cheque. But sometimes she looked tired and might speak crossly about how she had to maintain a delicate balance of their affairs and not relax, and how it was always she who had to make the decisions.

51
The Point

Although they stayed down at The Point at all times of the year, Robert remembered most clearly his summers there with Georgina and the children. Certainly everyone enjoyed walks along the beach when the wind was cold and grey, or his reading to them from a novel in front of the fire while the seagulls fled before a storm outside, but The Point was a symbol of his first summers with Georgina, and summers became a time for Robert to renew his acquaintance with his family. He saw how distinctive were his children's personalities, and how their brown limbs grew before his eyes. He did not have to snatch moments to talk to Georgina. They made love.

And Robert worked in secret at his craft. He liked to walk along the beach with an icecream from the shop, trying out the voices and gait of characters from books and life. With Georgina out of sight somewhere in the house, the children probably swamping another sandcastle somewhere and the year's lectures completed and all his essays marked, Robert stamped over the dunes, one foot after another, a rhythm carrying him on.

52
Silly Old Moo

Mrs Allynson came onto the verandah at The Point, collapsed in a chair, and moaned. Behind her was Mr Allynson with a basket of food and presents.

"Darling, could I have a cup of tea?" said Mrs Allynson. "And an aspirin?"

In the kitchen Robert and Georgina shook their heads at the image of Mrs Allynson, more and more like an old woman every day, working herself up into a state whenever she went on a long trip in the car with Mr Allynson and then subsiding and reaching for a pick-me-up as soon as she arrived. "Poor old thing," said Georgina.

"How have you both been keeping?" said Robert as he took the tea and a plate of cakes out to the verandah. Mr Allynson slapped his big hand on Robert's back and the children's heads, delighted to see them again.

At five o'clock Mrs Allynson got into a state again. She nudged Mr Allynson and said, "Laurie, it's time we went home," and because he could be a bit deaf sometimes she said sharply, "Dad! Come on!"

Mr Allynson was fond of the British comedies on his television set. He winked at Robert and Leigh and said, "Silly old moo."

53

CONCUPISCENCE

When Robert's father turned fifty-nine he became self-conscious about his appearance. He started to grow his sideburns after Georgina teased him one day about being old-fashioned, but then he went several stages farther. He bought jeans, a belt, a corduroy coat with leather elbow patches, and rimless spectacles.

And one day Robert caught him holding hands with young women in an anti-war march. Robert often saw his parents in the distance at these marches, and usually they were with Bill Prior and the others from the local Branch, but on this particular day Mr Saxby was by himself. Robert waited until the marchers had dispersed, allowing time for the look of fulsome concupiscence to leave his father's face, and then he made his way through the crowd and poked the corduroy shoulder. "This is good to see, the old pater doing the right thing."

Robert had the children with him, Leigh on his shoulders and Rosie holding his hand. They were excited about this chance meeting with their grandfather and held out their arms to him. Mr Saxby hurried them off the street and into the nearest cafe for a cup of coffee. He had a hunted look.

54
SPIRITLESS

Everyone in the Department was encouraged to attend conferences, staff-development seminars, in-service days and short courses. Career versatility was the talk. Keeping in touch.

Robert set off for a large and busy conference in another state. By the end of the first day he felt tired, lonely and paralysed. On the second day he sat up in the back corner and didn't know what they were talking about. On the last day he left early to catch his eight o'clock train. He checked in his luggage and walked through the streets near the station, wandering in and out of saddlery shops, dusty tap and washer shops and discount shops with perilous stacks of strange useful plastic things, and twice he hurriedly left adult bookshops, although he was fairly certain that all his colleagues were flying home.

At six o'clock he sat in a cafe eating a hamburger and drinking black coffee from a cup with a glued handle. The newspapers in this city wrote familiarly about crime bosses and Opposition Members he had never heard of, and in his briefcase there was a magazine wrapped in brown paper that he would read in his sleeper compartment on the train. He did the crossword, wiping pocket fluff off his pen. He wondered where the customers, lining the counter on stools, chatting to the man behind the counter, came from, and where they went when they slid off and left with their change or smokes or chewing gum, calling out goodbye. Perhaps back to the storerooms in the dusty saddlery or plumbing shops, or back to boarding houses. When the cafe door opened there was always a bellowing bus starting from a stop and rubbish blowing about the base of parking meters.

Robert left at half-past seven. At the station he waited for the platform gates to be opened, avoiding the mad eyes of a plump young man with urine stains on his trousers who was talking to people about God. The fellow made Robert feel anxious and he wanted someone motherly to come along and claim him, take him home and put his trousers in a washing machine and give him good food until his face became less like wax.

Robert wanted to go home. He missed everyone very badly. The young man reminded him of Gower. After each conference paper this week Gower had asked wild, embarrassing questions, and at luncheons he liked to lean close and say, "Things aren't going too well with my private life." His confidences worried one young woman and offended another.

Gower was exhausting to be with, his distressed face weaving too close to everybody and his confidences gusting into their polite ears in the corners of rooms. None of this was easy to put up with, although once or twice in the past few years Robert himself had wanted to talk about Georgina in the manner that Gower was talking about his own wife. Thank God I didn't, he thought, as he witnessed Gower's apostasy and apologies, his spiritless face in the evenings, always on the verge of asking for a cigarette or buying another drink. Robert thought that if Gower were to ask, once more, "Can I bot a smoke off you?", digging into his pocket and proffering twenty cents in payment, he might suddenly push at the recreant face and yell, "Stop it, Gower; snap out of it." But Robert could hear in his voice a note that was too high, tinged with his own uncertainty — not the no-nonsense, faintly irritable voice that Georgina might use to someone who was being silly.

55
THE BEST MIND

Robert was relating an anecdote to Eleanor one day, about an adventure that Rosie and Leigh had had with the little girl who lived two doors down in Degraves Street, when he realised that he had absorbed an enormous amount of knowledge about life in his street. Georgina was away at a session with the other editors and that fellow she talked about from time to time, Alan, the man the magazine retained for advice on the legal problems that arose whenever they published things that should have been checked out first. Eleanor was visiting, as she often did when things got her down. Robert and Eleanor kneeled together where the lawn bordered the footpath along Degraves Street, their hands in gardening gloves, weeds piling up nearby. Robert sneezed achingly.

"Bless you," said Eleanor. Her face and arms and legs were soft and brown from the sun, but she had flesh that bruised easily and only her beautiful hair leaped with life.

The postman stopped and looked down at them, holding out a *Newsweek* magazine. "Thanks," said Robert. "Nothing else for us today?"

The postman riffled the edges of his bundle of letters as though another letter for No 18 might thereby announce itself. "Better luck next time," said the postman. He seemed to disapprove of handing mail directly to his clients: Robert had noticed this before, had observed it when the elderly people in the street, with nothing else to do but garden and wait for the post, hovered behind their hedges with secateurs and stepped out to snip determinedly at some errant growth just as the postman arrived, turning to him in surprise as though they had been so absorbed they had forgotten about the post being due. "Hello there," they would say. "Another day, another delivery." Robert and Georgina had moved to 18 Degraves Street eight years ago and the same postman had been delivering to this area for years, or so someone had informed them. He always walked ("Never blows his whistle," said old Mrs Wright), rolling and pitching down and across the street because of one stiff leg ("He was in the war"), his black boots shiny, his blue uniform shirt tight across his comfortable shoulders. No one knew his name.

Mostly young families on the way up lived here. On the mornings when he did not teach, Robert looked out of his study window and saw the young mothers pushing their prams to the park or the shops. Sometimes two or three of them would meet and talk, peering under their pram hoods to determine evidence of life or to brush away flies, straightening up to exchange aspects of their lore. Robert was reminded of when Georgina used to take Leigh for a walk in his pram once a day, Rosie following them, infuriatingly slow because she had to crouch down and study everything. Her favourite was dog shit. Whenever Robert took the children for a walk the young mothers were uneasy. He had found himself explaining why he was sometimes at home during the day. Georgina, too, was a little disquieting to those mothers with their first baby. They were still finding themselves and there was nothing that Georgina, with her pram, baby and toddler needed to learn from them.

But that was years ago. Leigh was now eight and Rosie twelve — and Robert and Eleanor had finished pulling up the weeds. Pebbles and dirt and bits of grass had to be swept up.

A neighbour's little dog on an errand stopped to observe and got excited by the broom. "Oh, piss off," said Robert, laughing. Tigger growled in a bright-eyed way, his jaws clamped to the straw. Everyone knew Tigger and kept an eye out for him. He occupied himself with checking the street and visiting other dogs and houses. He ran his nose along the footpaths but lifted his head before entering a garden to say hello. These visits lasted for a minute or so:

he had a lot to do. He stayed longer only if something was out of place or new.

Another four dogs and at least eight cats lived in Degraves Street. They were the pets of the children who lived next door, across the road or farther down the street. Every day the children of Degraves Street surged out of their houses to play, either with or without a dog or protesting cat.

Robert observed the way that a child would seek to dominate the others, how young ones tagged along or were told to go away, which child had to sweep the path regularly or go for the milk or bread after school, who had lollies to give, who was learning to play the piano or the violin. They were all strict about friendship and defined its terms scrupulously, giving clear reasons for adopting or rejecting each other. This appealed to Robert: he liked to say that friendships had to be worked at. "But there will always be someone who lets you down," he would say.

Robert observed the way that hate and love and cruelty surged randomly in the children in the street. Once he used to intercede in their struggles but he soon realised that the children scattered and disappeared after his little lectures and judgements, the street would be quiet for the rest of the afternoon apart from a self-righteous taunt or a pet being called for its dinner, and he saw that he was meddling with inexorable things.

He kept his meddling closer to home. Rosie he loved: she was always busy with something, bouncy and clever around the house, precise and fearless with strangers. Unfortunately he felt ambivalent about Leigh, and sometimes behaved badly towards him, which wasn't right, but he did, and he couldn't help it. Leigh was moody, and sly about his friends and what he did after school. He spoke too loudly, mumbled his replies and thought too slowly.

One day a mother had rung to complain about him. "Well, what about it, son?" Robert said when he put down the phone.

Leigh was probably a few inches taller and weighed a few pounds more than the other boys and didn't know what to do with the extra flesh. His voice rose, shrill and quarrelsome. "Well, you tell them to leave me alone," he said, his face contorted with frustration, so that Robert felt sorry for him.

He confided in Eleanor that Leigh was a handful. "Like my husband," she replied, brushing small pieces of grass off her skirt as they went inside. They stood in the lounge-room doorway.

"See what I mean?" said Robert.

He walked quickly across the carpet to where Leigh was playing with his electric train set. "Right, young man. You're running over moths again, aren't you? You've developed a cruel streak. I don't know where you get it from."

At that moment Georgina arrived home. Waving to Eleanor, don't get up, stay there, she sat down, extended her arms and legs in relief, and told them about the lawyer who looked after the magazine's legal matters. "Alan's got about the best mind I've ever come across."

56

PROMPTING

One warm summer evening, the children decided to perform a play in the living-room for Robert and Georgina. It was the story of a princess stolen at birth and raised by a large, ugly family of villains and thieves. Rosie played the princess and, by cackling like a crone, draped in a blanket off the spare room bed, she also represented most of the members of the bad family.

She was the brains behind the play and had devised a story in which scenes of the ugly crone, hunched in a blanket, rubbing evil schemes together between her greedy hands, alternated with scenes of the fair, often-sighing princess, incomplete without love, forlornly fingering Georgina's brightest, filmiest, silk scarf. Rosie was quick and smart, adding bizarre twists whenever she got bored with the received version, devising dialogue that allowed the crone or the princess to leave the scene by way of the door to the passage or the door to the balcony overlooking the garden. Behind the appropriate door she had placed the blanket, the scarf, pots and pans, a tiara, a broomstick, a sword and a velvet cape. Some mosquitos came in from the garden but Robert and Georgina, cuddling on the settee, did not want to spoil the show.

Leigh needed quite a bit of prompting. He played the King who roared out in fury and promised his kingdom; Igor, the crone's ill-defined associate in mean, criminal poverty who had to be told to keep his hands to himself (at this point Rosie gave them a lewd look); and the handsome prince.

The kiss of recognition in the last act was a hit and miss affair. Also, the princess appeared to undergo a change of personality: she was obviously the princess because she wore the bright silk scarf instead of the blanket off the spare bed, and her voice was as the nightingale's, but she refused to melt into anyone's arms and apparently had learned something of power and high-handedness from the crone. The audience and the prince shuffled uncomfortably at this meddling with form but at least in the second-to-last scene the prince got to finish off the crone with a thrust right through her gizzard.

Leigh, in his wooden way, even managed to improvise on Rosie's script. Rosie had not been bothered with accounting for Igor's absence, it was the sort of thing she would wave away with her hand, but Leigh drew his dripping sword from the crone's body and said, "Die, evil witch. I have just stabbed your henchman and now it's your turn."

Robert's faith in his son was renewed. At the start of the evening he had settled back happily with Georgina to watch his children, and he had felt an indiscriminate love and closeness for them all. But then he had found himself mentally snarling at Leigh. There was Rosie, bright-eyed, original, drawing her audience's eyes, but Leigh, as usual, plodded his way through, seconds and steps behind his sister, dull-witted and for Christ's sake needing to bloody wake up, come on, quick, out with it slow coach, what are you trying to say, close your mouth before the wind changes. But then the prince found inspiration and with a sigh of relief Robert stopped churning inside. He found that he had been holding Georgina too tightly against him. What made it worse was knowing that Georgina encouraged Leigh; she never criticised him. Robert kissed the top of her head and the audience disentangled itself to clap as the prince dragged the crone's body out to the balcony before coming back on stage, his bride leading the way.

The actors bowed. Rosie's smile was for her father: acting was a link they shared. In the bottom drawer of the bureau Robert kept a scrapbook of programmes, posters and reviews of Ivan's plays from his student days, photographs of himself in costume, and photographs and production notes he had written for the plays he put on with his school groups in the days before he joined the Department. Rosie liked to bring these out and get him to talk about what he had felt and thought then. These days she was rather touchy about anyone kissing her or putting their arms around her, and she was full of scorn about most of the things that Robert said, but when she sat on the floor with him and asked him about Ivan and his own ambitions, she was dreamy and sentimental about his hidden depths. When she said she could not understand why he had ever given it up there was reproach in her voice, and she might say, "It's not too late to start again, Dad." Her eyes would be bright for him.

And so now she stood holding hands with Leigh on the living-room rug, bowing deeply, her smile abundant, carrying all before her. Robert missed having those feelings.

In her peaceful, growly way Georgina congratulated

the children, giving them brief, fierce hugs and insisting they pose for photographs. Robert's wife was slow to boil but her feelings were deep and lasting. Robert was rather noisy whenever he showed his love; his emotions were on his skin for all to see and they seemed to leak into the air. But it's love, that's the main thing, he thought. Families need times like this once a month or so to keep them together.

57
The Things He Should Have

One day Robert happened to go into a branch of his bank in an old working-class suburb. He had been thinking that he might be an actor again, or write a play, a play with a freak in it. Georgina didn't want to sit in the car and came in with him. He stood with her in the queue, catching his face in the mirror-window of the manager's office, Georgina aware of her reflection too as she stood chatting with him about things that earned them looks.

The queue moved along and Georgina said something, as she had done once or twice before recently, about the expert her magazine retained for advice whenever it got itself into a mess: "Alan's got the best mind I've ever come across." So you keep saying, your cunt practically wet with the thrill and importance of it all. Robert loved her full skirt, her glossy hair pulled back. He liked the way she narrowed her eyes in a considered frown. Robert wore his leather coat and expensive trousers and shoes. They were like a royal couple, except that no homage was paid; there was only a soreness and patience from the people in the queue, bent, bloated, shrunken or old from lead in their systems and starch in their diets and no cheer in their jobs. "I'd like to invite Alan and his wife for tennis at The Point next week," she said. "Do you mind?" The things he should have nipped in the bud.

58

DIFFERENT SHADES OF DARKNESS

In the early years after they had bought The Point, friends had come down in summer for weekends of tennis and swimming. Most of them had been Georgina's friends and Robert disliked many of them. He disliked that side of Georgina that could want to jump about and laugh with such satisfied, convinced people. He hid in armchairs with a book but they always found him, and so he played stinging games of tennis, making them run around the court until they grumbled something about let's have a drink. "Was that really necessary?" Georgina would say, settling a tray of drinks on a table under the Moreton Bay fig tree.

The games had lapsed as more and more of these friends divorced and remarried and their children grew up. Sometimes no one except Mr and Mrs Allynson came down to see them. Robert and Georgina busied themselves with other things — books, apple orchards to visit, a trip back to the city for a meeting or lunch or whatever, the hedge to trim, a walk along bush tracks instead of the beach for a change.

Mostly Robert found himself setting off alone on long rambles along the sand or following the coastline on the cliff tops, trying out voices, stopping to buy chocolate or milk at the little town nearby before walking back again, his head full of characters. He imagined himself in the shoes of freaks, misfits, heroes and villains from the novels and plays he had read. He spoke aloud the things they might say. Sometimes he explored the possible directions a recent argument or incident with Georgina might have taken. His feet slammed down on the sand-dunes. More and more often, Georgina liked to stay inside and read. Days might go by and her only excursion outdoors a walk to the phone box.

But now she was excited about renewing the tennis games. They drove down on the Friday night, leaving Rosie and Leigh at Degraves Street with orders to behave themselves, and got up early on Saturday morning to mow and roll the court and clean the house and make up a bed for Alan and his wife.

At ten o'clock their car arrived. Georgina and Alan kissed hello, and Robert shook hands. Clare, Alan's wife, stood scowling at them, and scowled while Georgina explained about their room and where the bathroom was. She scowled for most of the next two days. It was traditional to drink a lot but Clare drank very little due, Robert supposed, to a need to guard her tongue, not because she disapproved of drinking.

They played a game of doubles before lunch. Clare seemed to watch Georgina with an exalted, hostile look and once or twice Robert caught her looking fiercely at him. She turned neatly on her toes and hit the ball hard. Why do I want to put my arms around her? thought Robert. It doesn't make sense.

At lunchtime Clare tossed aside her racquet and walked into the kitchen to help Georgina. Robert found himself alone with Alan, babbling on about the magazine and Alan's job. He had one ear on the voices in the house. He heard Georgina's soft replies and the vigour in Clare's voice, and he had a sense of an estimating smile on Alan's face.

After they had eaten lunch under the Moreton Bay fig, Robert hoped that the others would want to sleep for a while. He went for a walk and as he returned he came upon Clare sitting on the edge of the cliff looking down at the surf. She did not look up at him but began throwing pebbles and grass stalks over the edge. Georgina and Alan were below them on the beach, walking idly and talking, stopping now and then to look at shells or to consider some issue. It had been years since Robert had seen Georgina so absorbed. He felt vaguely guilty about that. It was a hot day and he wanted to swim, but he turned around and went back to the house to read in the hammock Rosie had given him for Christmas.

At the end of the next day they had had enough of tennis and walking, talking and eating together. Clare sat on the living-room rug wearing headphones and reading a record sleeve. She had stopped scowling and looked tired. Georgina and Alan sat at the table finishing a bottle of wine. Robert thought that they looked generous and complete with one another. He tried sitting and talking with them but Georgina's efforts at turning her concentration to him were like those of a large ship turning upon the ocean. "Sorry? Can you say that again?" she would say.

He thought that he ought to let them find their own way through the mess, because anything he might say or do was beside the point. But, at the same time, he decided that he would take his study leave in Europe next year and take Georgina with him.

Robert went outside and sat on an old stone wall and scraped at a bare area of the ground with his toes until it was powdery. The stone wall and the ground were still warm from the day's sunshine. Ahead of him were different shades of darkness: the sky without many stars as yet, a darker silhouette of tea-trees and pine trees, and the sea below him. There was a lighted ship, probably a tanker, moving across the black water. He leaned down to scratch a mosquito bite on his ankle and sensed someone sit beside him quietly.

"Hi," said Clare.

He went on scraping dirt into a mound with his bare feet. Clare stretched out her foot and patted it down, restored it, and smoothed it flat again. Her foot looked like a bird poised warily at a pond, dipping its head occasionally, and Robert found himself scooping up dirt with his toes and sprinkling it across the bridge of her foot. He felt that they were about to grab one another.

"We're both hurting, aren't we," she said.

Oh Christ, thought Robert. He went back inside the

house. "Would you two like some coffee?" he called, as he walked through the house to the kitchen, his eyes straight ahead.

59
Lying in Wait

During the following weeks Robert had an uneasy sense of his behaviour being geared to encouraging Georgina and Alan. He suggested meals and visits to cinemas, or left Georgina and Alan alone whenever he could. He showed friendliness towards Alan, and went about his own work and home life with a busy air. I must be perverse, he thought. He felt an urge to provoke the crisis which he felt lying in wait for him.

Georgina began showing a range of signs that made him feel sick with dread. There was a soft, far-away look almost all of the time, a preoccupied manner when he was talking, a click once when he answered the phone. One afternoon, when she phoned to say that she would be late getting home, he heard the wires humming with the presence of someone standing near her. She was very busy; often there were meetings. They stopped making love: "The body can't lie," she said. She hated cooking but would spend frenzied lunchtimes driving to obscure delicatessens and greengrocers, coming home to cut her thumb at the cutting board, beside herself with anxiety because so and so, or her editor, or Alan and Clare were coming to dinner.

And yet she sometimes gave him smacking, tolerant kisses and friendly, unexpected cuddles. He hit his funny bone on the edge of a door and she said kindly, "You're a silly duffer, aren't you." He had become quite awkward and uncoordinated.

And the following day she might snap at him and the day after that screw her face up in remorse. Robert did not say anything to her, but he wondered if she knew that he knew what she was going through. She probably did, being Georgina, but she did not have the will to talk to him about it.

He thought that he would wait. He hoped that she might come round. He was tired of the way she was being inward, day after day, sitting somewhere with the cat in her lap, her eyes straying back to her book while he talked to her, sometimes looking as if she were in pain, as though he had been insensitive. They're good at making me feel I'm obtuse, he thought. The whole bloody precious lot of them. He asked her, "What's wrong?" and she would instantly look back to her book, one hand waving don't pursue it and the other stroking the cat.

But he loyally stayed in each evening, swearing to himself that it was always he who asked what was wrong and never they who volunteered it. He connected her with cats. She was oblique, watchful, devious and calculating. She had a face upon which love and self-love mingled. During the day, when he was at work, he thought of her, and always there was the cat in her lap as she sat, her eyes half-lidded, her long legs drawn up on a couch, her skirt mantling her knees, mild and impenetrable, saying no to something.

60

DOWN THE DECADES

Mrs Allynson often asked Robert if he had decided to do anything about his acting ambitions. "You could join your local drama group," she said. She liked to take an interest because she had played the role of a little curly-haired girl in a couple of films made when she was eight, in 1932. There did not seem to be any copies of the films available, but in the family papers that she showed him Robert found some studio stills, and on a crumbling poster that clearly showed her name there was her face peeping from behind the broad back of a man on a horse droving sheep. There might have been one or two other little films as well, but she couldn't remember now.

That was all that Robert knew about this aspect of his mother-in-law, and the romance of it was quite at odds with her face powder and grandmotherhood.

One day he arranged for the Department to borrow a documentary film about the Great Depression. Every year he gave a series of lectures about documentary film-making, and one of the lectures, which he called "Daily Life", was very popular with students and other staff members. Robert suspected that he didn't have much to say that was new, but the lecture theatre was always packed. He liked to think that people came to see him act. He drew on original diaries and letters, and he moved about, trembling, like an image on an old film.

On the day of the lecture, Robert played a skeleton-skulled man shuffling along in a ration queue, weighed down by an old greatcoat, rolling a cigarette with one hand. Then he was a fat capitalist out of a banned cartoon. He was Jack Lang, the rebel premier, casting about for favour and an edge on his opponents; a tinker selling shoelaces at the door; a woman coughing into her handkerchief.

He lectured for half an hour. His voice cackled, boomed and whined; it sounded hopeless and bitter.

After that he showed the film. It was a standard documentary, a measured voice narrating over one or two jaunty songs about moving on and going hungry, a few flickering seconds of dole queues, protest meetings and shanty towns, and politicians standing outside a public building, shaking hands, smiling a little too long down the decades.

And then, for about five minutes, Georgina's mother appeared. Robert knew that it was her. She must have been about eight years old at the time, he thought. He wondered how she was approached by the makers of that film, what explanations were given to her mother and father, and whether her actual mother played the role of the mother in the film.

The five minutes covered a day in the lives of two little girls. Georgina's mother played the role of the squeaky-clean girl, delighted, proud of her own good behaviour, doing her homework, eating her dinner, hopping into her bath, reading a book at bed time; and in each scene her virtuous little face was finally drawn to the camera's eye, which made her dip her head shyly with the thrill of everything. A mother's caring hands were always there to wash away the soap or tuck her in.

After each stage in her day the film cut to scenes from the life of a slum girl, whose day surged in fits and starts, random and careless. There was a hole in her dress and no shoes on her feet. The mother ladled a glug of something onto her plate and her grimy hand crept across the fissures in the table-top to pick up her spoon. Her white teeth and the whites of her eyes were bright in a gloom that came from a lack of electric light and soap.

Robert closed the lecture by referring to the present economic crisis. For three minutes he condemned a world in which too many people grew up without knowing enough about their many peers who lived mean, curtailed lives. His finger pointed at the dead, white projector screen and he almost spat a couple of his words.

61

THE UGLY DUCKLING

Robert's children grew up to be at once unfamiliar and tiresomely constant. Rosie was nineteen now and had finished her first year at university. After Christmas Robert drove her back to the city from The Point to collect her exam results. He waited in the car, watching her walk up to the neighbour's front door to collect the mail being held for them, wondering what he would say. But Rosie gave a typical Rosie squeal and dance on Mrs Lizacic's doorstep and ran back to the car crying, "I've passed! I've passed!" She stopped and clearly enunciated, "I am now going to fucking well wipe myself out." Robert kissed and hugged her.

Rosie seemed to have the world at her feet. She said she'd stay in the city for two days and celebrate with her friends, see how they'd done, and could she have the car please, she wouldn't wreck it or get picked up or anything, and he could take the bus back to The Point, okay? All year she had shut herself away from having a good time, she was tired of being one of the swots, it was time she raged a bit, okay? She turned up at The Point four days later, fresh and blooming despite her claims of drinking orgies. Many of her friends came down to visit. Boys Robert had never seen before started hanging around. One boy, Michael, stayed for six days.

Rosie was renewed; she looked with fresh interest at the things around her. She hugged Leigh. "You're getting spunky," she said. "You're not the ugly duckling any more."

Robert looked on in surprise, and realised that it was true. For years Leigh had made a demon uncoil inside him. For years he had had to curb his snideness and irritation with his son's slowness, his lack of wit and grace.

But now the clashing elements of the boy's body were harmonising. He was quite tall and he glided unconfined among people, chairs and tables. Girls liked him and he was breezy with them. People seemed to want to rest their fingers on his arm or chest. They were drawn to the hard planes of his face. He had stopped being a bully, though he seemed contemptuous of shorter, older, less fit, less intelligent people. Robert saw that women and girls sometimes seemed overcome by his son's energy. They faced away from the impatient thrust forward of his thighs when he walked up to them or stood close to them.

That summer girls from the houses at The Point finished their half-day in the milk bar or bakery and stood on the front steps of Robert's holiday house mumbling through chewing gum: "Is Leigh here? I was wondering if he wanted to go for a swim." It was pretty obvious to Robert what was going on, and there was a part of the beach that he avoided when he went walking.

Robert found it unnerving coming to terms with his son's sexual attractiveness. It didn't seem so very long ago that he had been on at the boy all the time about any weakness he could find. He felt mean-spirited about that.

And later in the year Rosie announced that she was going to move out of her university college and live with Michael. Georgina did not seem to mind but Robert felt that probably they all should talk about it a bit. "Who is this Michael bloke?" he said. "How long has this been going on? You didn't tell us. Do you know him very well? He could easily just walk out on you, you know, leaving you high and dry." The family was a little short with him and he retorted that he did not know if he could justify continuing Rosie's allowance in the circumstances. But it was just a matter of getting used to the idea, and by the time Robert and Georgina left to go overseas on his study leave he was even calling in to Rosie and Michael's place to say hello.

62

LUCKY DOG

At twelve o'clock one Friday there was a staff meeting, and at one o'clock Maggie and the others took Robert across to the Staff Club for lunch and a send-off. Six months study leave, you lucky dog. A colleague and his wife would live in Degraves Street while they were away, the bills had all been paid, Leigh's board with a neighbour accounted for, Rosie and Michael had had them over for dinner last night and, before they flew out on Monday, that left only Georgina's send-off at the magazine and dinner with Alan and Clare.

Maggie was a little sentimental with Robert on their walk to the Staff Club. She squeezed his arm and spoke vivaciously, only breaking off to exchange greetings with the students who called out to her, "Hi, Dr Thiele."

Flanked by their friends in the Department, they entered the Staff Club. Last year the university had built this new Staff Club on a site near the swimming centre. For a couple of weeks before the landscaping was completed, everyone had had to walk along springy planks, two inches clear of the mud, to get to the entrance. Late on a Friday afternoon in winter Robert had seen Ted Gower stop as he left the Staff Club, dither while he got the planks into focus and, with a small defeated yelp, hold his trousers at the knees and wade through the mud. Two awed students helped him climb out. Gower had promptly set off for his office, walking his tiny-paced walk on his tiny muddy feet, pulling his head into his roly-poly shoulders in boozy contentment, withdrawing one hand from his coat pocket and occasionally taking draughts from a silver flask. And now, in the small foyer of the Staff Club, he had just collided with Robert.

"Six months, eh? Lucky dog."

Maggie leaned on the hatch in the doorway of the commissionaire's alcove and signed in one of her Honours students, Sonia something or other. "We should give her some tutoring in a year or two," Maggie had been saying to Robert recently. But now the commissionaire was bobbing at them, using their full titles and surnames. Behind Robert, Gower called, "What's worth sinking the old fangs into on the menu today, Dick old son?" and the commissionaire jerked out a democratic, "Dr Gower, sir. Haven't seen you in here since yesterday at least. Now, would that be a liquid or something more solid you had in mind, Dr Gower?" Good old Dick. There was hearty laughter. Gower, what a prick.

"Drink first, sweetie?" said Maggie. Robert walked to the bar with her. He watched her put her hands on the edge of the bar and lean forward so that her elbows pointed out. She looked nice today; he could call her his best friend. As if recognising this, as if reading his thoughts, Maggie turned around and said, "I want plenty of letters from you while you're away. Long ones. This place is going to drive me insane in any case, but a nice newsy letter will be almost like talking to you and it might delay the process." She handed drinks to everyone, murmuring, "John, yours was a beer, Ted a red, Anton, Sonia... Well, cheers everybody, here's to Rob's study leave and his six months of comparative sanity." Robert silently toasted a return to comparative unity with Georgina, imagined them both unwinding together away from all the distractions. "And if we think he's going to be casting fond thoughts in our direction we've...got some more thinking to do," said Gower with a shout. Gower always launched himself well.

They stood in line at the servery, peering into the stainless-steel food reservoirs. Robert chose veal cutlets in cheese and breadcrumbs. Maggie looked at it disapprovingly. "Had that yesterday. It was cold inside." This made him feel anxious. He piled a side plate with salad and picked up three butter pats for his bread roll. He felt tired before they had begun.

There were eight of them farewelling Robert and they made a boisterous table in the far corner. Maggie hailed a waitress and ordered wine. They ate and drank like condemned people. Robert looked curiously at Sonia, Maggie's student. He supposed that she felt left out and overwhelmed by them all, and probably would not have come if she had known the purpose of today's lunch. She left early. "Charming girl that, charming girl," said Gower. "Rob, old chap," said Gower later. "Could I, ah, prevail upon you for a...um...cigarette?" Gower was fumbling inside his pocket for a coin to give him.

"Sorry," said Robert, pulling back from the twenty-cent coin Gower was pushing through the crumbs and salt-shakers to him, "gave up years ago."

"Right, right, I remember now. I wonder if..." Gower looked around the table.

Maggie was dispirited, her face saying to Robert, You get study leave, I get Gower.

Maggie, Gower and Robert left at five o'clock. Robert took advantage of a screen of students and whisked Maggie behind the poplars by the swimming centre. They watched Gower wait, blink around for them, and finally scurry away across the grounds to his office.

They walked slowly to the car park. Maggie said, drunk and confiding, "What do you think about having affairs with one's students?"

"You're kidding. Do you mean Sonia?"

Maggie swung her satchel around and hit him on the hip. "Of course I don't mean Sonia. Just shut up and I'll start again. What are your views on having affairs with one's students?"

"Come on, I'm not going to accept that. Tell me who it is."

Maggie tossed her head and walked ahead of him saying lightly, "I try to have a talk about a hypothetical issue and all you can do is get all excited about details."

He caught up with her and after a while she put her arm in his.

"Does Brian know?" he asked.

"It hasn't happened yet," she said tiredly. "But it might. But I might not feel like it when the young man in question gets up the courage. Or I might have to take the initiative. Or I might be overcome with guilt at being unfaithful to Brian and not be able to carry it through."

"Don't think about it too much," said Robert.

63

TABLEAUX

When he got home Robert showered and changed into a suit. Georgina's magazine was giving her a send-off party that evening, starting with cocktails and champagne in the office and finishing with dinner with Alan, Clare and one or two others in a nearby bistro later. Georgina had come home to change, and while Robert was dressing she talked about the interviews and other small assignments that her boss had asked her to carry out while she was in Europe with Robert.

"It'll be fun," she said. "You don't mind, do you?"

"No. Of course not. It'll be nice. We can work together perhaps, help each other out."

"Well, I don't think so," said Georgina. "We'll be doing quite different things. While you're doing your research and tracking down your films I'll be..."

"Look, I only meant it will be a nice feeling working together, having a holiday together, both of us with something to do, we can talk over our work with each other, we can..."

"Yes, well, that's all in the future, isn't it? We'd better go, Robert."

Georgina drove them into the city in her car and parked it outside her office building. In the foyer, the lifts and the reception rooms were enormous grainy photographs of models dressed in wool for winter. Some models were alone; others were in tableaux with men and cars and mansions and dogs. "We'll get you a new suit in London," said Georgina in the lift on their way up. She looked as flourishing as a model on a poster.

Georgina took him to meet her new boss. Robert was feeling grumpier by the minute. He did not want to meet anyone new. Her boss was a picture in blue: his safari suit was a pale, powder blue, his shoes were expensive blue pumps with tiny tassles and his hair had touches of a grey that was almost blue. When he said hello to Robert his teeth showed white, momentarily lightening the bluish tone of his dark, shaven jaw. He looked to Robert to be out of touch and out of place. But later Robert warmed to the man, as he watched him gravely, courteously dispense the drinks and talk to his staff who, with their disobliging, dissatisfied faces, were busy putting one another in the shade.

Robert told himself to recognise his own grumpiness for what it was instead of feeling hostile towards people who did not deserve it. He looked sourly across the room. Alan was talking to Georgina, as he had expected. Robert had been feeling tense ever since Georgina had told him about the party a week ago. He knew what to expect, and despite his efforts to glance disinterestedly around the room his eyes met Alan's each time and were received with an annoying smile that he was sure hid darker facts. Alan was a man people admired without hesitation.

Robert shook his head in wonder at his own behaviour. Why had he been actually encouraging Georgina to invite Alan, or Alan and Clare, to dinner, drinks, films, plays? Every couple of weeks, it seemed, they all did something together. And everyone went along not saying anything about what was going on. And now someone was standing at his elbow saying something to him.

"Talk about your fashion plates," said Clare. "They could sack the models and just photograph each other. Georgina's wearing a lovely dress. And how's Leigh? Did you find a place for him to board while you're away?"

Clare tended to jump from subject to subject like this. She smiled at him. He was never sure what her mood would be.

"Oh, yes. Yes, he's staying with a neighbour," he said with an effort.

"Georgina really does look lovely tonight."

They both looked at Alan and Georgina across the room and were rewarded with a wave. Instantly Robert and Clare turned to each other, not wanting to appear to pry.

"You're a bit out of sorts about things, aren't you," said Clare suddenly with a look full of meaning, nodding her head briefly at the other half of the room. "Your body language tells me this." Her smile was like a fatalistic sigh, with kindness and humility in it.

"I wanted to rush screaming into the night," said Robert to Maggie on the phone the next day.

64
THREES

Georgina was warm and unhurried with him during their holiday, touching him and folding into him, her eyes always half-lidded. In London she took him along to get fitted for a Hardy Amies suit, afterwards holding onto his arm wherever they went. She might have sneaked in one or two letters or phone calls to Alan while they were away, but when he was in bed with her in a hotel or *pensione*, it was easy for Robert to think that she had not.

But he felt that he was losing touch. Somewhere in Wales he saw a man sitting on a stile and, when he mentioned this to Georgina, she said, "What on earth are you talking about?" They had a picnic in a field. A Harrier jet cracked across the sky, and Robert sensed that some tiny people had flattened themselves under the hedgerows, and he sensed them stand up again, clamorous and enraged. Outside old buildings he caught ducking heads and swirling coat-tails in the corners of his eyes. The summer in Europe that year was cold and discouraging.

It had to do with threes: three figures marking his progress, three choices to make, three disasters and three triumphs together. They came upon a village tucked into a gap bound by a creek, the road, and some cropping fields of a manor house. The stone houses were damp and grey, animated into villagehood by a child, a woman and a man standing far apart from one another. They came to a wayfarers' junction. There were three roads out: one over a stone bridge embellished with carved faces gorgonised by wear and tear, and two others leading dimly somewhere. He wanted to take the bridge.

He stopped the car to let Georgina drive. "Where now?" she said, but there were no milestones to consult, just two plinths on a lean in their collars of grass, a goat on a rope ignoring them and some stone blocks and broken slate that might once have been a coach-stop shelter. Robert felt dulled by landscapes and did not reply. "Well, I'm going over the bridge," said Georgina, turning the steering wheel and letting out the clutch, snicking a couple of pebbles at the legs of a woman waiting there with suitcases as though ready to come with them. Robert saw her unremitting expression, and on their way over the bridge he looked around. She was still staring at them, raising and lowering her suitcases as though in offering. He fancied that he could hear her fretting. "What woman?" said Georgina, adjusting the car's heater. "Where?"

65

Breathing in Hopeless Air

When they got back from Europe, Robert had six days of his study leave left. He decided to drive down to the beach house to work on his notes and catch up on his reading. Important books were always coming out and he wished that they would stop for a while. Georgina had things to do in the city and was to drive down a few days later.

The drive down to The Point made Robert feel deeply depressed. As though tracking with a camera mounted upon rails, he could see the past, see the Galaxie travelling through patchy flat suburbs with their corner milk bars, see the dry grass and pram wheels on the undeveloped lots, and back walls of houses criss-crossed with laundry pipes. When the children were growing up winter had seemed to be a perpetual condition in those places: they had passed unfinished houses on muddy lots and read daily advertisements in the newspapers pointing out their modernness and desirability. The journey to the beach house had taken an hour and a half in those days and, Robert found, still did, and the children in the back seat of the Galaxie had turned fretful and bitter, as though breathing in hopeless air.

When Georgina arrived later in the week they decided

to go for a walk along the beach. She had forgotten to bring quite a number of things with her, for some reason, and so she put on his old fishing coat, and three pairs of socks so that his hiking boots would not be too loose. She searched through the cupboards and found one of Leigh's old beanies. She pulled it down over her ears and put up the collar of the coat.

They climbed carefully down the cliff path to the beach, talking about the coldness of the wind and the tans they had acquired in Greece. The problem with coming back in the middle of the year, Robert thought, is that the season is winter, the country is hugging itself and everyone at home is confirmed and steady. He felt nervous. He had been hazarding guesses at what Georgina had been doing in the city, what she had been saying, what decisions she had been making.

Slowly they walked to The Point. There were eddies of scum in a channel that ran through the sand and into the scrubby trees behind the dunes. They had to leap across at the narrowest part, while on the other side a fisherman with poles and fishing baskets waited impatiently for them. They raised their eyebrows at each other after they passed him. A tendril of Georgina's hair was a startling colour against her face and the greyness of the air. There were three fishermen on the beach. Beyond them was The Point. Seagulls slipped down planes in the air, sometimes snatching up fish from the waves. Georgina was silent and Robert could not bear it.

They heard a thrumming in the air. The third man was sitting on the sand playing three manic red kites tied to a steel bar, and he was forcing the kites in awkward angles up, down and across the sky. They walked behind him to avoid the glinting wires that controlled the kites. Not that the man noticed them or even seemed to care: or perhaps he did notice them and was affecting disinterest. He was sitting stolidly, his self-absorbed, bearded face looking ahead, moving only the steel bar that he held with the mechanical claws that he had instead of hands. Robert and

Georgina could hear a creaking of leather and Robert fancied that some socket or strap was taking up the strain under his coat sleeves. Blankets were tucked around him. He did not have any legs and they did not know how he stayed upright. A stern woman and child sat in a hollow in the sand dunes a few yards behind him, staring fixedly out to sea, waiting for him to finish.

"That was weird," said Georgina when they were safely past the group. She was very shaken. They walked together, with their heads down, to the other side of The Point.

The red cliffs beyond The Point were corroded and lumpy, and the table of rock was sharp and treacherous. Seagulls stopped to look, or sideslipped in the wind. Robert felt cold. He could not see clearly, as though it were snowing. His ears were hurting with the cold and he was thinking about the branch that had cracked a window of the sunroom last night. He put his hand on Georgina's arm as though to stop her from beginning to say: "You no doubt know Alan and I have been seeing each other. We want to live together. I don't know how else to say it. I'm sorry, Robert."

66

Live Like That

After their twenty years together, Robert was not quite able to believe that Georgina had gone. She seemed still to inhabit the house; at the edges of his sight and hearing he kept catching her shadow, her dress swirling around a door, her light, quick step in one of the rooms.

He began to invent reasons for not going out, made food last to spare himself shopping trips. It was a time for concealment. He read many novels, finding, in their characters and situations, connections with his own state. Irritating advertising jingles ran through his head and he felt cold all the time. He grew to hate shaving and sometimes left it until late in the morning; until prompted by the thought that someone might visit him. He washed his hair every day, unless it was lying flat when he woke up and not fluffed up like a surprise. His bed seemed especially empty at night. When he put on his clothes he looked in the mirror and made small adjustments to what he was wearing, thinking that he was still an attractive man but that it was sad there was no-one to tell him so.

He walked for exercise, stamping across the neighbourhood park to the beat of recriminations that were intended to leave Georgina (if she had been there with him) forlorn with contrition. The only people he met in the park were fathers on fortnightly access to the children, or Nat, the little boy from next door, who talked to himself.

He thought that it was no good telling himself that depression came in cycles and that all he had to do was wait for a cheery fortnight to come round. His life had slowed right down. The house felt hollow, but he worked quietly at the minutiae of daily existence, keeping busy, keeping everything clean and in its place. He thought about letting a couple of rooms but decided against it, knowing he would have to sell Degraves Street and move to a smaller place soon anyway.

He spent a certain amount of time each day on his lecture notes, refining his thoughts before he began by stacking papers parallel to the desk edge and laying his pencils, pens and the gold letter-opener Georgina had given him side by side, graduated according to size. It occurred to Robert that he could measure his days by counting beats: one, two, three before the gas flame caught alight under the kettle, five taps in from the margin when he was typing something, letting the telephone ring ten times before acknowledging that the person he was ringing was not home — or perhaps not answering. He worked very efficiently, shaping his life by listing on note-paper the tasks that had to be done and crossing them off one by one. But once or twice he caught himself listing and crossing off tasks that he had already completed. He hated the look of that note-paper unless it had a satisfactory ladder of firm strokes through *bank*, *ring Maggie*, *mark essays*. He put all his books in alphabetical order.

He cooked a different meal every day: fish in a wine sauce, mushroom curry, blobs of minced steak squashed into hamburger patties, quiche sometimes or a fancy omelette, stuffed peppers, tuna mornay, his mother's egg-and-bacon pie recipe, leftovers on toast for lunch.

It was no good. The letters and phone calls from Georgina never came and, in waiting at home for them, he missed out on important family and social events. He began to accept invitations.

He thought about the people he might have to talk to, and realised that he had not said a word to another person for three or four days. "Hello," he said, testing his voice in his empty house. Then, just before he was due to leave the house to go to these dinner parties or drinks, he would shower and shave until his face was tight and expressionless, and try on several combinations of coats, shirts, ties, trousers and shoes, liking none of them, feeling dowdy in all of them. He took a long time to dress, often dropping things and looking at them for a long time before picking them up again.

He went out to buy new clothes. Georgina always did that when she felt depressed. But it was a paralysing experience. He trudged around the city's expensive little shops until his feet ached, and then around again because he had forgotten what a colour or cut was like, convinced that everything he had liked initially was in fact unfashionable, too dear or cheap and nasty in cut, and then he would go home with something that he hated from a bargain basement.

He looked at his friends and colleagues with gloomy interest afterwards, feeling convinced that what he wore was never quite right. One of the things he missed most about Georgina was the loving intimacy of her familiarity with his favourite things, the way she knew what clothes he liked wearing, the colours she said looked best on him, his weakness for certain things.

He hated catching sight and sound of Mr Saxby in his own actions. His conversation was rhetorical, his nose trumpeted, he had recurring baldness dreams. Although he might have been called middle-aged, his hair was still thick and he wore it in the style of the times, but he had a dream sometimes in which he ran his hand over a warm, bony dome, faceless people murmured things which might have been slighting and mirrors dogged his days with close-ups. When he woke up he found himself alone and quite intact, but still, he felt uneasy after these dreams, convinced that something had been removed from him in the night.

Robert dreamed of the stage, Mr Saxby still dreamed of printing beautiful books. They both were waiting. Robert joked with his children one day, "If I get like my old man when I'm his age, put a bullet in me, will you?"

"Are you looking after yourself, Dad?" Rosie asked.

Robert shrugged and hoped that she would not pursue it. He did not want to explain how he had worked out a system to stay healthy. For a start, he would not cut himself off any more. He would go out and meet people. And he would look after his body. He reckoned that a game of tennis after work with Maggie, or taking the long way through the park to the milk bar, would obviate the need for any further exercise on that particular day, or even the next if he should spend the afternoon in the garden as well. And exercise might help him sleep. There were nights in which he did not sleep but watched old British murder mysteries on Channel Nine, thinking of others in the city who might be watching television at four in the morning because they were old, or ill. He did not want to live like that.

67
Boom Boom

He slept with someone called Anne for two consecutive nights in which nothing happened except that he oozed emotion everywhere and scared her away. There was a grim, mechanical time with someone else, who backed off, sore and violated, saying miserably, "I want to go home."

On his first morning with June he found her looking pensively at a tampon left behind in his bathroom cabinet, and a few days later she teased him about a pink handkerchief. Georgina's hair clips seemed to start emerging from odd places now that another woman was spending time at making his house a home.

June adopted a comfortable air of proprietorship over his things. When Maggie and Brian visited him soon after he met her, he saw them watch her walk across the room to look for something in a drawer and they heard her ask him, "Are you cold? I'll get you your brown jumper." She stacked away the dishes, announced that it was time she was in bed and turned to them and said, "Nice to have met you." On the way back from the bathroom, toothpasty and her makeup removed, she placed her finger to her lips and pressed it against Robert's forehead and whispered, "Don't be too late." Good old Maggie and Brian, keeping in touch with him during this rough time, keeping up his spirits with these visits, looked at each other, obviously thinking, Who was that? How long has this been going on?

Robert wondered if he was either not ready for love or too ready for love. Things with June declined and before long they both began to delay and avoid: they discussed whether or not he'd stay the night if he happened to be at her place, and, in bed, whether or not they'd screw before going to sleep.

Gillian lived in a flat near the sea and was getting ready to move north to a warmer climate. Robert began to calm down. He would stay at home for the first part of the evening, before going around to her flat to meet her when she got home from waitressing at eleven o'clock. He avoided looking at her *Vogue* magazines and *The Prophet* on her coffee table, her book of coloured photographs of children's smiles from around the world, her incense sticks.

She was inspired by risks. She liked to make love to him in front of the open fire, alert for the return of her flatmate. She liked to make it interesting. She dressed in a nightie and instructed Robert to wear only his tracksuit top and leave the bottoms laid out flat on the thick rug by the fire where he could get into them if they heard the key in the front door. They stood face to face. She pulled her nightie up to her waist, glanced at the general area of his forlorn knees, snorted and collapsed back onto the couch. Robert stood before her, filled with emotion.

"Not yet," she said, her voice muffled behind her hand. She struggled to restore some order to her face. "First we'll have a trial run."

She simulated making love with him and suddenly smacked his bottom hard. "Now!"

He had to do a backwards roll onto the floor, lie on his back, shoot his legs into the waiting track-suit pants, the elastic waist band slapping him about a bit on its way, and finally settle under a blanket in an armchair by the crackling fire and frown at a book in his lap. Something had scratched him.

"Five seconds!" yelled Gillian. "One more practice run!"

Eventually they had a long, dozy time in front of the fire, one ear open for the sound of the key.

One night in bed in the dark he leaned on his elbow and said, "Your nipples are a bit dry and chapped. You should put some cream on them." But they both had drunk too much and he could not get much sense out of her. She fell asleep, turning on her side and butting backwards into his lap.

In the darkness of the early morning he said, "Your nipples are a bit dry."

"Pardon?"

"You should put some cream or something on your nipples."

Gillian took his hand away and touched herself.

"Oh Christ!" Her feet shot out and a toenail scratched his leg. "Oh dear," she said. "You poor thing." In her agitation her head jerked, smacking his jaw.

She pulled and twitched around the bed. Slowly she recovered from her giggles. "Take me, take me," she said, and then collapsed again, doubled over, and blew a trembling raspberry against his stomach.

"Well?" he said resentfully.

"Oh dear," she said panting. "Whooo!" She collapsed onto her side, exhausted. He irritably connected her silly giggles with her choice of books and knick-knacks.

"Look, all better," she said, and in the gathering light Robert watched her peel a thin membrane of sticky tape off each nipple.

"It's that dress I have to wear at the pub," she said. "I hate my nipples pointing out."

When she finally moved north Robert was plunged into telling Maggie everything, all the time.

"Stop it, Robert," she said. "I don't want to hear any more. I think you're being silly."

"Maybe," said Robert gloomily, thinking of Gillian and others like her. He thought that he liked them best when they were about to set off for work. "See you," they called. They stood at the door and looked back into the house, waiting for him to come up and kiss them, yesterday's dress or jeans folded into a compartment of their briefcases or cane baskets. They stepped close to him, standing on his feet, digging their hands into his pockets as though to say these are my pockets too, looking up into his face, wriggling a bit. Boom boom.

"Mmm, bye," Georgina had always said, after a

spirited kiss and a brief melting against him, a tumble of busy keys in her hands, gloved in winter, fresh toothpaste, shampoo and perfume smells eddying in the swirlings of her abundant skirts and capes and hair, the odds and ends of car-driving and the day's business bundled in her arms, her hair disordered by her upturned collar; or trimmed of all this in summer, a couple of simple filmy things covering her, her legs and arms bare and sandals on her feet, and a purse, a paperback and a bathing suit in the open cane basket. Shit, shit, shit.

68

Advisory

Family and friends were a safer bet.

He sought out Maggie to play tennis with him; when he partnered her at doubles he found himself letting her call "Mine!" or "Yours!" and take all the risks. He was dreamy, plodding and uncoordinated, sliding in the gravel uselessly and causing them to lose too many games. "Concentrate, for Christ's sake," she would say.

In the Staff Club afterwards, or on the verandah of her house on Sunday afternoons, she brought him glasses of beer and shook her head. Robert seemed to bump into table edges and door jambs all the time these days. He once said to her, when she looked in dismay at the glass he had just dropped, "It jumped out of my hands."

He sought out his sister. Eleanor's youngest child was a boy aged four, and she always fluttered around him in nervous devotion when Robert visited them. She seemed to keep a cloth permanently in one hand, alert for anything the little boy spilled or smeared. She made coffee for Robert in the kitchen, her eyes smudged with tiredness, her head cocking as though to an inner voice but in fact she was deciphering crackles on the intercom connected to the child's bedroom.

Just lately she was more open about what she had been up to. There was a man, but she did not know if he would want to stick around. She explained:

"You know when you're obsessed with somebody, can't wait to see them again, can't get them out of your mind, you almost ring them dozens of times a day and if you do ring and they're not there or the phone's engaged you just about climb the wall, or you speak for hours, totally besotted, everything's a fairy tale with meadows and everything, you know; but then you hang up and see the kids' mess everywhere and the kitchen benches have got laminex tops and who's going to want to take you on and where are the *kids* all this time you're walking hand in hand with someone in some meadow with your shoes off? And the rules. First rule, don't fall in love, then make sure you define all the terms, never write a silly letter, always be well informed about the wife's movements if he's married."

She told Robert that having or looking for a love life was hardly worth the strain for someone in her position. Not only did the thrilling telephone stress how prosaic were the colouring books and her daughter's eye infection, but news of her single state travelled and weirdos came out of the woodwork. "These guys, friends of Colin's, men I used to work with, men I hardly even know, come around or ring me at eleven p.m., thinking I'm a fair bet now that he's left. Or they ring and don't say anything, there's just this creepy presence that practically seeps into the room with you, and then they hang up. I've got a pretty good idea who it is. Twice he's rung the door bell at night: the first time there was a bunch of flowers there and the second time that *Eleanor Rigby* record. If I didn't have the kids perhaps men wouldn't do these things to me."

Robert developed an earache and called in to see his brother at his surgery. Geoffrey gave him a prescription for ear drops and seemed afraid that Robert might be depressed and want to unburden himself. Robert watched his white shirt cuffs rustle across the green leather border around the blotting paper on his desk top as he wrote out the prescription. Geoffrey always wrote with an expensive gold fountain pen, held precisely in his clean, pale fingers. His thin lips were austere and advisory. Robert and Geoffrey had last seen each other on Christmas Day, and it would be the next Christmas Day before they saw one another again.

Robert visited his parents more often than he had done in the past. Mr Saxby was semi-retired. On the days he didn't go to his workshop he followed Mrs Saxby around the house, or watched her put out snail bait in the garden. In the kitchen he asked her, "What's that you're cooking?" If she went out in the car he peered out of the window until she returned.

"Dad," Robert would say, "how about a round of golf?" and he'd wait while Mr Saxby said, "I'll just see what your mother wants me to wear." Mrs Saxby had retired. Her friend Bill Prior had died last year. She told Robert, "I have to get out of the house or your dad will drive me crazy," and so she taught English to migrants for a few hours each week. "Do you know," she might say in an undertone, "I was having a wee yesterday and your dad came in while I was there and said, 'I just wondered where you were'!" Leigh and Rosie often urged Mr and Mrs Saxby to go overseas for a long trip, but Mr Saxby said, "I wouldn't know what to do with myself."

Mr Saxby always wore the old corduroy coat when he played golf with Robert. Many of its honey-coloured ridges had worn away, and his rimless glasses now had a chipped lens and no longer rested comfortably on his nose. Robert could not understand how his father could see out of such a cockeyed mechanism. Unfashionable sideburns seemed to pull the flesh down from Mr Saxby's skull, gathering it in stubbly jowls which bunched over his collar when he turned his head to gaze at another of the young women whom Robert had been bringing along with him lately.

They played very slow games of golf together. Mr Saxby did not like to hurry, preferring instead to settle in for a good yarn after each stroke. He was very considerate and did not ask what Georgina was doing. Other golfers gathered behind them and soon asked if they might pass.

If the golf course was fully booked they walked across to the park near the Saxbys' with their golf sticks. The formless thickets and tangled wire and picket fences and squeaky swings and slides of Robert's childhood had been swept away by progressive councillors. He felt that his past was being eaten up before he had properly finished with it. He chopped at the cropped grass with a golf stick.

69
FRIENDLY, CALCULATING, POINTLESS

In March of the new year the students returned. They clasped the open door of Robert's office, their brown limbs idly swinging, wanting to do his course. He looked at their enthusiastic grins and white teeth and felt wretched and sybaritic. He went looking for love.

He looked at the girls he taught, or the girlfriends of the boys he taught. He flirted in a circumspect way, amused and irritated to see that they instantly were on guard. He would say, with an embracing wave in the pub or after a class, "Can I give anyone a lift?" His arm brushed against them. He was always interested in what they said. He announced that he needed some notes typed. He went to bed with two or three of them and had a friendly, calculating, pointless time, and never a word was said again. He hoped that they would not fall in love with him. Maggie watched all this, almost expressionless, as though to tell him he should be taking her glances as a warning to think about what he was doing. Maggie, as constant as the daylight. He hoped that other people did not think him foolish. He often told himself that he would just like things to be simple for a change.

70
COME-ON

"You've really been putting out this term," said Sonia, to tease him. "All that chatting up and fingers brushing together kind of stuff. All those jokes in your lectures. All that come-on stuff."

Robert's face twisted and he thrashed about in his chair. "Has anyone noticed?"

"Maybe Maggie has, but she wouldn't care. Anyway, it's no-one's business."

She reached across and took his agitated hand.

"Actually," said Sonia, "because of the pittance the Department is offering me to teach a measly two tutorials a week I've been thinking I should see the job in terms of getting screwed."

She smiled at him and he couldn't bear it. He didn't know that hair could be so black. He reached over the table and touched her head.

This was their first time out together. They had declared themselves. They went on to tell one another their histories and their plans and their likes and dislikes, about their previous affairs, misadventures with sex, and other disasters, telling little lies in order to find comforting similarities of taste and interest, Sonia saying "David" and Robert saying "Georgina" casually as names of people once important to them but now only vague presences at the edge of their lives. It was almost like a preparation for a future together.

71
FROM THE INSIDE

Robert saw Rosie once or twice a week now. She was training to be a teacher. Sometimes he brought Sonia with him to lunch and he was pleased that Rosie liked her.

Rosie was bright and appealing to be with most of the time and Robert was careful to avoid the two subjects that would set his daughter off: Georgina-and-Alan ("You're well rid of her, Dad") and the allowance that he gave her ("It's too much, Dad, I can't pay you back"..."I don't want you to pay me back, sweetheart. As a father I want to do it"..."It puts me in a position of obligation to you, like I have to visit you regularly or do something in return, even if I didn't want to — don't get me wrong, Dad, I *do* want to visit you, it's just that"..."I *want* to do it, sweetheart; I give Leigh the same amount. I want to make things just that little bit easier for you both"..."Well, one day I'll be in a position to return it").

Instead they chatted about the trip to India she planned to make with Michael at the end of the year, or her approaching teaching practice.

"I can't sleep, Dad. I wake up Michael in the middle of the night and demand a massage. I go and make hot milk and honey and brandy drinks. I go for runs and go to the gym to tire myself out. Falling asleep's no problem, I just wake up at two o'clock or something."

"You'll be all right," said Robert. "Don't let them see you nervous, know your stuff, have plenty of alternative activities for them."

"It's not like when you were at school, or even when you were teaching. Kids these days are different. They're monsters. I just know they're going to send me to a tough school and give me the roughest classes."

When Rosie spoke with feeling about schools and education, Robert felt uneasy. She was knowledgeable, condemnatory and sincere. She felt she could achieve something, however small; it was only the thought of fronting up to her first class that terrified her. She gazed at him sometimes, made her statements, gazed again, and Robert hunted about for something to say in response. He could not hide his ignorance about his profession, or his years of indifference, or that he must appear to her a sinecurist. He hated it when Sonia was there too, gazing at him, waiting for his response.

"I don't know why you didn't keep on with your acting after university," said Rosie suddenly one day. The three of them had met for a counter lunch.

"You're joking," said Sonia. "Did you used to act? You didn't tell me that."

Both were alive to the possibilities, and it occurred to Robert that he had lost his spirit, had done so a long time ago, that Sonia and Rosie recognised that there must have been something that moved him once and they wanted to see it in him again. Perhaps it did not matter what it was, just so long as he was moved by something that lit up his eyes.

72

THE PROBLEMS OF THE DAY

When Robert suggested going to The Point for the weekend, Sonia said, "Since it's not far from my mother's weekender cottage, let's call in on her. She really wants to meet you." Robert wasn't sure if it was such a good idea. It was like putting a seal on things, meeting her mother, but that wasn't the kind of thing he could say.

Miriam walked out to greet them when they arrived, kissing her daughter and then Robert, afterwards holding on to each of his hands and stepping back to smile at him. She was dressed in a brocaded blouse and a tumble of full, bright skirts and petticoats, and wore gold rings on three of her fingers.

She sat them down at a dark work-bench in the kitchen, urging wine and cheese and salami on them as she chopped up things for lunch. The work-bench was a massive slab of wood scored and burred all over its surface, reminding Robert of his childhood, of the counter in Simpson's, the butcher's shop where he had bought scraps of meat for Gypsy. He watched Miriam slicing and peeling and thought about various things: how age differences did not matter unless you found that you had to teach someone things because they were so far behind you; how Miriam and Sonia bubbled away, all their senses agitated, appealing to be with but so unlike Georgina, whose manner was slow, neutral, assessing. Robert hoped that Miriam didn't find him too much like a forgettable, middle-aged man, a man too old for her daughter, a man who was half-hearted about the problems of the day — especially since she, and her daughter, and the people who he supposed normally came down here, had a flair and a commitment which they wore like second skins. He mentally shook himself to concentrate on Miriam and Sonia's conversation.

Later they walked to the dam for a swim. Golda, Miriam's collie, dashed through the grass ahead of them, snapping at butterflies and turning in circles to rid herself of a piece of grass clinging like a salute to her head. When it became clear to him that Miriam and Sonia would not be wearing anything, Robert swam naked too.

73
GENEROUS IMPULSES

They went to see films or went out to dinner, skied, hired a boat from time to time, lived together on and off. But Robert was careful to ration his time with her, believing that she might grow to like him too much. He did not want to meet her friends: he could not rely on other twenty-two-year-olds being as quick and wise as Sonia. When she talked about her past he listened with half an ear, thinking that it was unimportant compared to his twenty years with Georgina. He explained to her his caution, his need to be often alone.

And so the rules grew, and he could see that Sonia was baffled. She had once said, blushing with embarrassment, that she thought he might teach her something about living her life, and each time she came upon a particular form of his bloody-mindedness, Robert could see her innocently wondering what lesson she should be noting. Patterns repeat and lessons are learned. Robert found himself explaining things to her, hearing in his voice the tone and words that Georgina had used when she was explaining something to him, and he heard Sonia use the words that he sometimes used.

"I don't know where I stand in all this," she said finally.

"Well," said Robert, as though about to start numbering on his fingers, and he grew expansive with the lessons of life. He said that life is a long process of losing the generous impulses of love. "Being unhappy has made me act badly," he explained. He said he thought he was becoming a nastier, more impatient person: he snapped at shop assistants, the television repairman, other innocent people. He described a chain of learning linking its way back into the past and ahead into the future, and how victims of love visited their warped and brutish lessons upon their new lovers, thereby creating new victims.

"And so," he said, "I've been ruined for love. You must protect yourself. I'll only stuff you up."

"You're really full of shit sometimes, Robert."

74

Drained

On the day of Mr Allynson's funeral, Robert left Sonia at home, and Georgina left Alan at home, and Mrs Allynson acknowledged Robert as the senior, responsible male.

It was a cold morning. Georgina wore a dark coat and a black silk scarf at her throat. She looked sad and tired and gave him a grateful smile. He chided himself when he realised that he was thinking that neither of them would play games today, nor give out even the tiniest flicker of recrimination; and, he told himself as he caught her perfume, this was no time for thinking that he still was in love with her.

Georgina and Mrs Allynson sat in the front of the car with Robert. "Laurie wouldn't stop talking about the visits you made to him in the hospital, dear," said Mrs Allynson. "You made his last days happier." Robert had a feeling of past family occasions as his arm brushed against his mother-in-law's when he changed gears.

A hushed, fervent man came down the steps of the undertaker's building, clasping his hands and bowing towards them. He opened the car door and fussed as they got out. "Would you like to see your husband, Mrs Allynson?" he asked. "He's in the chapel." He turned to Robert. "We find that the final glimpse allows the family an easier release," he whispered, as a young man took Joyce Allynson and Georgina along a corridor. "You'd be surprised how important it is to see the loved one actually in the casket and know it's a final stage in travelling on." The undertaker stopped and they watched the two women walking ahead of them. He seemed to want to explain the theories of his profession. "A psychologist at a convention I went to last year gave a paper about it," he said. "Much better than having one's last look in a hospital bed or hearing they've been mangled and killed in an accident and never seeing them again." They walked a short distance and the man stopped Robert again. "We can usually make the body presentable, but," he said. Georgina was looking back at them and making cross little gestures. "I think your wife is wanting you, sir."

The tiny chapel had plaster crucifixes tipped with gold paint and a thick carpet and weak piped music deadening the scrape of women's stockings and the squeak of Robert's best shoes. Georgina's mother looked down at her dead husband. Mr Allynson seemed even smaller than he had looked in hospital. His face looked pinched and chalky, his nose patrician. The glossy wood and the silver handles drained him of colour. "Poor old fellow," said Mrs Allynson. "Poor old fellow." Behind them, the rest of the family filed in.

75
TABS

The Saxby family was the sort of family that keeps tabs on who has died, had children, married or divorced. Robert's Uncle Max rang him to say that he was getting too old to be the family chronicler, and would Robert like to do it? Robert said he would, and a few days later Uncle Max arrived outside Robert's house, got out of his car, grunted his way towards the back seat and backed out cautiously with the family Bible and a few papers clasped to his chest. "It's all in here, boy," he said, tapping the spine of the Bible with a long, cloudy fingernail.

It was not: for the next two weeks Uncle Max posted Robert envelopes containing hasty notes on vellum paper, butcher's paper and the margins of newspapers, many of them confusing, plain wrong, or repeating word for word an earlier letter. He received a murky photograph of the mayor of a northern city, and in the margin Uncle Max had written: "Your Aunt Alice was once betrothed to this chap." One letter, that Robert presumed to be sent by mistake, implored the board of an old, austere bank not to let itself be taken over by some upstart or he, Maxwell Saxby, JP, would have to consider selling his shares. Luckily Mrs Saxby was on hand to help Robert make sense of Uncle Max's version of the family tree: she seemed to know just about everything about the family. Finally, just before he gasped and died at a shareholders' meeting, Uncle Max sent Robert the family photo album.

Uncle Max had collected an odd bunch of photographs, including one of his bowling-team captain, and he had never managed to get more than three corners under the black, gold-edged tabs that kept them in place. Only one photograph in the album had any connection with Robert, and that did no more than hint at his existence. It was a tiny photograph of his parents. They were standing on a crowded railway platform, his father dressed in an army uniform, his mother leaning against him, her hair like Rita Hayworth's. Someone had scratched the date in ink on the back of the photograph: January, 1940. Robert calculated that his mother had been pregnant with him for at least a month at the time the photograph was taken. Apart from that Robert thought that he could see his own thin mouth, neat head and cautious eyes in a photograph of his great-great-grandfather, husband of a cross-looking woman and father of two little girls, in pinafores with tumbling hair, and a dull-looking little boy. A lawyer or a doctor, thought Robert, but another photograph showed the same man dressed in a shopkeeper's apron.

With his mother's help Robert made a meticulous record of the family's material and emotional fortunes. He collected photographs of his parents' first house, the untidy house that he had grown up in, with the new white Holden parked in the driveway; baby, school and graduation photographs of Robert, Geoffrey and Eleanor; Georgina before and during their marriage; their two children; a nation-wide family reunion of fearsome unknowns organised by Mr Saxby some years ago; Robert's mother and father finally outside 10 Downing Street, and his mother and father being buried in the sand by Robert, his bottom bony inside gingham bathers, the dimples on either side of his spine revealed to the camera like large, soft eyes as he bent over his parents to shape the sand over their knees.

The job of family chronicler became a burden to him. Whole tribes of nephews and nieces announced their wedding dates or the birth of their children, and Mrs Saxby always had something new to tell him about his peers, their divorces and remarriages. He wondered if he would ever have any more details to add to his own line. At the same time he was called in by Mrs Allynson to help her with the records that Mr Allynson had been keeping of the Allynson clan. One day she said, "I suppose we'll be adding a new line for Georgina and Alan soon," caught herself with a gasp, and blushed. "Sorry, dear," she said, and rushed into talking about Leigh's twenty-first birthday which was coming up next July, saying she supposed Robert would be taking photos for the record.

Robert thought that things had lost their order, even the Saxbys' tendency to produce a new generation every twenty years at the start of a decade. He liked the symmetry of Grandpa Saxby being born in 1900, followed by Mr Saxby in 1920, and he himself appearing eight months after Mr Saxby had boarded a troop-train that would take him to a training camp in January, 1940. He married Georgina in 1960; but Rosie did not marry or bear in 1980, and Leigh would be twenty-one soon, on a cold day in mid-decade.

76
WAY OUT

The months went by and Robert thought about Sonia. They spent their weekends at favourite parts of the coast, stopping at favourite pubs for a drink. In the lounge of a pub, at a lightless table next to a wall of dark glass windows, in a quiet corner where spotlights distributed the shadows, Robert thought: she is twenty-two and I am forty-seven and Georgina is forty-six. She is bouncy and self-conscious, I have baldness dreams, and Georgina is cool and unassailable. She had doubts, and I have some doubts, and Georgina has never had any. She makes simple, mistaken connections about things and I know they are mistaken because I know more and I have faith in what Georgina would say in similar situations. I express something and Sonia will respond, or I will try to unravel her random comments on some theme, and suddenly we both stop talking and sit upright, each looking at the other seated way over there, the baffled face way over there; and I used to be able to finish a thought of Georgina's almost before it had taken form.

He hunted through his voices and roles for a way of conveying this to her. He didn't want to be evasive. He went into the subject of Georgina at some length, pointing out to Sonia that so far things had been a series of small disappointments for her; and, he concluded with a twist of his mouth, she would be better off with someone else; *he* had been ruined for love. (This was the best way — help her to find the way out. Encourage her to do something definite — but ensure that she comes out of it feeling some tenderness and understanding for him.) "I'm really sorry," he said with feeling, coming to the end of his explanation.

"Don't look round, but that little shit Gower just sat down over there with some woman," said Sonia.

Robert frowned with effort. "Sorry?" he said.

"Dr bloody Gower. He's sitting over there behind you."

Robert did not move. He could imagine recognition seeking domination over other emotions on Gower's face, could feel Gower waving at them to join him.

"Play dumb," said Sonia. "One mid-life crisis is enough for me at the moment without having to encounter a walking embodiment of it as well. Why hello," she said. "Taking in the sea air for the weekend?"

Gower stood at their table, his hand outstretched, almost about to retreat. It took him some time to accommodate Sonia and her question. "I beg you pardon? Oh, no, no. The wife and I drove down here this morning. Her mother had to go to hospital — we're just visiting." He asked where they had been for the day. Robert explained. Gower ignored Sonia, kept his eyes almost averted from her. He was disturbed by her. Suddenly Sonia dropped her hand onto his forearm and suggested, in her intense way, that he try the lobster salad.

"It's wonderful," she said, "fresh and delicate."

Gower, unmanned and shaky, seemed to struggle with her face. "Miss er, Miss er..."

"Call me Sonia."

"Sonia. Yes. You...I seem to recall..."

"Yes?"

"I'm sure I've met you before," said Gower in a rush.

Sonia sat back and considered him. "That's quite possible. Let's see...Perhaps at the staff meetings we have every Friday at twelve? Or in the Staff Club every Friday lunchtime and some other days as well? Perhaps in the Department office or one of the corridors at least once or twice a day, two days a week, all this year? I know — perhaps in your office a few weeks ago when I asked you to come and speak to my students about the special subject you're offering next year."

His face flushed, Gower pulled back and stood up. "You can't expect me to...we have a high turnover of ..."

"Idiot," said Sonia, losing interest.

Her contempt seemed general and Robert had a temporary feeling of connection with Gower.

77
DOG

On Monday morning when Robert went into the Department to collect his mail, he saw Gower in the corridor pinning a cartoon from *Punch* to the door of his office. Robert nodded hello and continued on to his own office, but Gower quickly sidled across to him, his elbow nudging. "Well, what do you know," he said. "You sly devil. Sneaky dog."

78

SEND-OFF

In November Rosie completed her teacher-training course and she and Michael began packing and re-packing for their trip to India. "How long do you think you'll be away?" asked Robert. Rosie sighed happily and slapped her thighs. "For as long as I feel like it," she said. "A year? Two?"

    That night Sonia suggested that they should give her a good send-off, invite lots of her friends down to The Point for the weekend. "I'm sure they won't want you and me down there," said Robert, "but I'll ask her."

    "Great," said Rosie on the phone the next day. "Love to." On Friday night, she said, groaning down the telephone to him, she had to go to Georgina's and Alan's for dinner, a real drag, but she and some friends would come down on Saturday morning in Michael's car. "We'll have eggs and bacon and coffee ready for you," said Robert.

    On Friday morning Robert went into the city to buy presents for Rosie and Michael. He discovered that he knew almost nothing about his daughter's needs or preferences and cared little for Michael's. Michael smiled upon everyone; he liked to explain the spiritual aspects of massage. Finally Robert bought Rosie a camera. He bought Michael a copy of *Siddhartha*, remembering back years ago to the tastes of his students who had been along the hippie trail. Michael seemed no less a profound little shit.

    At lunchtime Robert and Sonia drove down to the beach house. They told each other how they were longing for some peace and quiet before the hordes descended the next morning. Mrs Taylor, the Department secretary, had let it be known that she could not finalise the results sheet until certain people had finished their marking. "Monday at the latest," she had said. Robert also had a thesis to assess and three references to write. They made a small fire in the evening, when the air got cooler. This was when they liked each other most, when they were away from the Department for a few days, working quietly together, stopping to discuss a point that might emerge from a student's paper.

They were still in bed when Rosie, Michael and their six friends arrived the next morning. Robert made bacon and eggs for everyone, wearing only his track-suit bottoms, extracting all he could from the initial pauses and looks as his daughter's friends took in this older man and his young girlfriend. Sonia played her part to the hilt, too, wearing a thin t-shirt over her black underpants, combing her tangled hair with her fingers, yawning and smoking on the old couch, and finding, in her sleepy voice, that she had friends in common with one of Rosie's companions. Robert looked on with a smile.

The bacon and eggs ran out quickly and Robert said that he would walk to the shop to buy some more. Two of Rosie's friends came with him. They seemed fascinated by him and wanted to talk, and he enjoyed hearing them discuss their studies and future plans. The morning was sunny, heavy with spring smells. The gravel crunched under their shoes. Robert felt blessed that he had a happy, well-adjusted daughter with cheerful, open friends. The day was perfect and his heart was susceptible.

They all went for a walk after breakfast, straggling out along the beach as far as The Point and back again, and had coffee and read books in the sun afterwards. "They really are nice kids," said Robert, percolating the coffee. Sonia looked faintly irritated. She seemed to be summing him up more than usual, and held her feelings more in check — which was exactly as he had advised her to do, but still, there were times when he had needs. "Yes, Grandpa," she said. Deflated, Robert took his coffee to his hammock, but two youngsters were rocking in it and all the deck chairs were taken. He put a vinyl bean-bag on the verandah and promptly felt perspiration wetting him.

The events of the day repeated themselves, and only

dinner and the coming evening held the promise of making everyone feel wide awake again. Robert drove to a fishing town to buy crayfish, disappointed that no one wanted to come with him. He saw himself making a sauce for the crayfish and a dressing for the salad, pouring champagne coolly while the ignorant boys stood by, all elbows and pimples, the young girls watching him pour and looking with longing at a drop of water that had run out of his shower-wet hair and down his lean face. He began to feel a little better and practised a speech of farewell for Rosie and Michael.

Something of the kind did happen and he felt that the balance had been redressed. After dinner they lit candles and drank Benedictine with their coffee, talking about Asia for Rosie's and Michael's sake. Michael sat on the floor, rolling a large joint and saying several very silly things in answer to silly things said by some of the others. Robert decided that Rosie still had a way to go, and his eyes pricked with sentiment. He wondered if Georgina ever sat down with the friends of Alan's children like this, but his attempts to picture it failed. Sonia sat on the floor between his legs, rolling her head and shoulders under his massaging fingers. He found himself listening very closely to her, pleased that she did not seem quite as young as the others. Two or three went to sleep in their armchairs and Rosie took Michael's head in her lap. No-one could be bothered to drink or smoke any more, or change the record.

Robert said a few things about spare rooms and plenty of mattresses and pillows for those who need them, and see you in the morning, not too early please, and Sonia and he were going to bed. But the bathroom was occupied and remained so for hours and he had to lie in bed in torment until he could be sure everyone had gone to bed so he could have a leak in peace. He returned to his bedroom. There was a boy in the passage, tottering back from a closing door, a fuzzy look of shame and thwarted lust on his face. Robert recognised the look and the emotion; he was surprised to see them in the present generation.

On Sunday morning Robert and Sonia drove back to the city so that the others could have some time on their own. Rosie stood by Michael's side, smiling peacefully as she waved goodbye, and Robert felt a tug at his heart.

79
DINNER OCCASIONALLY

A few days later Georgina rang Robert to say that she had seen Rosie yesterday, and heard about the nice weekend everyone had had at The Point, and this Sonia sounded very interesting, and she had just thought to herself that it would be nice to have dinner with him soon. They settled for the following Friday. He had heard that the La Salle was pretty good.

"Fine," said Georgina. "That's settled. See you then."

"How have you been?" babbled Robert into the receiver. "How's things at the magazine?"

Since it was a cool evening and a smart restaurant, Robert put on the suit that Georgina had bought for him in London. It was a beautiful suit, a dark, expensive suit, and when he had worn it in London Georgina had stroked the lapels and sleeves. If he wore the suit now it would tear at her a little, make her remember things, cause a twist in her heart.

While he waited for her he tidied around the house, his heart tumbling. Degraves Street was a big house and he liked to say that he rattled around inside it. Leigh's old bedroom, Rosie's old bedroom, this and that unused room, marks where pictures had been removed, indentations in the carpet, books on a slope in the bookshelves. Georgina's solicitor had written saying he had been instructed by his client to inform Mr Saxby that the sale of the house could wait indefinitely until he, Mr Saxby, had made other arrangements. "Well, fucking bully for you," Robert had said, crumpling the letter but smoothing it out again to put in his "house" file. He tidied the newspapers, brushed his teeth after his coffee and thought about a brighter tie.

He imagined how he would open the door and give her an easy smile. Enough time had elapsed. He had things to do, she had things to do, dinner occasionally.

He opened the door in an unconcerned way when she finally arrived, smiled, and said, "Nice to see you." He had time to notice that Georgina's smile was uncontrolled around the edges before she kissed him and rested her side against him. She clapped her hands on his hips, stepping back to look emotionally at his suit and his face. Robert stored this away. He was anxious to leave for the restaurant. "Are you all right here?" asked Georgina, looking past him into the house. "Are you looking after yourself?" She walked in, glancing around her at the uncherished walls. She stopped, turned, and put her fingers on his chest: a familiar gesture, one that reached his heart, and he thought, rue the day. All this was bad for him and he did not believe it and he wanted to be going. His actions large and cheery, he held both her wrists, clapped her hands together and said, "Let's go, me old love. I'm starving."

Out in the street he held open the passenger door of his car for her, looking back at the red Mercedes sports car parked behind his as she gathered her skirt in one hand and got in. "New car?" he asked.

"Don't even talk about it," said Georgina. "In hot weather it boils all the time, on cold mornings it stalls. I tell Alan I'd be better off with something sensible."

Robert got into his car and turned the key but the engine refused to fire and the battery grew weary. "Flooded," he said. "I'll wait a few seconds and try again. Sorry about all the stuff on the floor."

"I've always liked the smell of this car," said Georgina. She leaned down and picked up a hair elastic. "I see," she said.

At that moment Robert tried again, the motor started and the car coughed away from the kerb. Robert's grin, as he concentrated, was wide and unwise.

They parked the car and entered the La Salle. "Bonsoir, monsieur, bonsoir, madame," said the waiter who took their order. "What?" he said, bending and reading the menu over Georgina's shoulder. Flawlessly she repeated her order, pointing to the menu while the waiter mouthed and wrote down the syllables. They waited. Eventually tight little garlic mushrooms came for Robert and he picked at them while, across the room, a loud man explained to his guest that he had developed a consensus of scenarios to help him deal with the crisis-type situation affecting his firm's output, production-wise. Georgina, her face collapsing in endearment, mumbled, "It's nice to see you. I've been thinking about you lately."

"That's nice. I've been thinking about you, too."

"Sonia...is it serious?"

He shrugged. "We get on well," he said, to keep things ticking over.

"Do you think you'll ever get married again?"

"Don't know. It's possible."

"Does Sonia want to get married?"

"I don't know. We'd get on well," he said.

Georgina looked at something past his shoulder.

Robert said, "What about you?"

They were each doing a lot of shrugging.

Robert had a feeling of holding his breath. He waited, and then asked her how she was getting on with Alan. She said vaguely, "All right." As though to shake off her mood, she suddenly began to talk brightly about how nice it was having Leigh staying with them while he was between houses, about her small car accident recently, Leigh's new girlfriend, the death of her cat, all the things that once he would have been the first to know about. And there were other things, too: dinner recently with Alan's friends, whose names one saw in the paper, and how she was updating Alan's *Who's Who* entry, which, she said, was a bore. "I just can't keep up sometimes," she said. "I leave things to the last minute all the time. For instance, tomorrow morning I have to go in and buy a new hat for the Derby."

"Yes, of course you do," he said.

"Look, don't start," she snapped.

The waiter finally brought coffee and cheese, placing the cups and plates on the table with what seemed to be a terrible clatter and waste of energy.

"Do you think you'll get married?" asked Robert at last.

But Georgina did not want to talk about it. Robert could not work her out. All through coffee and cheese, and the drive home, and the stillborn talk in his car (she apologised for not coming in for a coffee), he heard the intemperance in his voice. After she had left he ran their conversation through his head, to help himself discard another impression — that she was used to something better now and that he had lost because his house was a little shabby, the restaurant they had been to a little careless, his car a little uncertain in its reliability. She had been keeping in practice, checking to see she had not lost her touch, making sure he was still there. He waited for a few days, and when she did not contact him again Robert put some of this in a letter he was composing in his head.

80
Sparse Sentences

On Christmas morning Rosie rang him from Bangkok and at eleven o'clock Leigh came to see him to exchange presents. Leigh was apologetic; he couldn't come to the Saxbys' with Robert because he had arranged to have lunch with Georgina and Alan. Robert sighed.

Leigh left at midday and Robert drove himself to Mr and Mrs Saxby's for lunch. Eleanor was there with her three children. All day she seemed about to spill tears and looked helplessly after her youngest child running riot. Robert waved to his brother, who was on the other side of the room. Geoffrey put the tips of his doctor's fingers to his lips. Geoffrey and Mr Saxby faced each other from deep armchairs, nodding into remote distances, their sparse sentences struggling to carry over the Saxby Axminster. At one point Geoffrey turned away from Mr Saxby and said to Robert, "How's Georgina? Do you see much of her these days?"

It's so easy to flatten someone, thought Robert. He looked at his mother's boarder helping to set the table. She was an unhappy girl called Theresa who taught in the school where his mother used to teach. She had no parents. She looked terribly nervous, and broke a wine glass. Mrs Saxby frowned at him to talk to her.

But then during lunch they relaxed when Mrs Saxby told her funny, sharp stories about the family, imitating voices and mannerisms, picking at sham. His mother, the family recorder. Robert wondered if she were intimating to Theresa that she would be better off without a family. Looking at Geoffrey saying, "Elbows," to Eleanor's children, and Eleanor's bowed head, he thought that Theresa had only to look around the room.

They opened their presents. Theresa had spent too much money on everyone. Eleanor went away somewhere to sleep. Geoffrey said, "Oh, mother, it's very nice, but I wish you wouldn't buy me clothes." Robert gave his father a book of bird plates, a limited edition of a beautifully made book, thinking that Mr Saxby would appreciate fine printing. Mr Saxby sat looking dumbly at the slip-case, fearful and reticent, his lap and ankles overwhelmed with wrapping paper.

"It's from me, Dad," Robert said loudly.

Mr Saxby looked wonderingly around, his liver-spotted hands fluttering.

"It's from me, Dad. Thought you'd appreciate a fine printing job."

Mr Saxby smiled brightly and said, "If I'd had time I

would've tried my hand at more of this sort of thing instead of forty years of leaflets and invitations."

Oh hell, thought Robert. Before leaving that afternoon he managed to get a smile out of Eleanor and Theresa, and he pulled open the sun-blind shading the windscreen of Geoffrey's big car.

On the way home he called in to see Mrs Allynson, who had just returned from lunch with Georgina and Alan. She clasped him to her. She looked much older. "It's lovely of you to drop in, dear," she said. "I miss my dear boy. Have you heard from Rosie yet? I got a lovely card from her from somewhere in one of those countries."

"This morning," said Robert. "And I'm taking Leigh to a restaurant tonight. First time I've ever been out to a restaurant on Christmas Day."

Mrs Allynson said, "I'll be by myself tonight. I can't stop thinking of Laurie. Georgina told me to stop being morbid, but he was my husband — I can't just suddenly stop thinking about him, can I?"

"No. It's only natural."

"It's only natural..."

They exchanged presents. She refused his invitation to have dinner with him and Leigh, but asked him if he would stay a while and help her sort out something in her chequebook. "Laurie always did the cheques," she said. "When he died I had to learn how to do it but sometimes I mess things up. Perhaps you could..."

Robert stayed for an hour and a half, listening to his mother-in-law's voice trail away at the end of each sentence as if she no longer expected anyone to hear her out.

81

CALCULATION AND CURIOSITY

A few weeks later Rosie returned from her trip to India, alone, looking wasted and fatigued. At Degraves Street she curled herself up in armchairs and smiled palely from her pillows when Robert brought broth to her room. She refused to stay with Georgina. "You're well rid of her, Dad," she said. "I can't stand that Alan person."

Michael came to the door one day and handed them a key and a camera bag. "These are Rosie's," he said. He scribbled on a piece of paper and wrapped it around the key. "This is my new address. Tell her she can have the doona if she wants to come and collect it, but the cooking stuff's mine." Sonia, of an age with this fellow, seemed inclined to want to chat to him on the doorstep about India, but he was in a hurry and her loyalty to Rosie won out. "I feel like a bloody parent," she grumbled, taking Rosie a book to read.

Rosie said: "Michael was so unfeeling. When I got sick he used to leave me in our scungy hotel room and go off and try and buy dope or do deals on the black market." Sonia and Robert perched on her bed, listening. "I was so lonely and sick, and he just left me alone all day apart from getting this weird doctor who squeezed my tits and told me to be careful about the water."

Robert had often heard from Sonia how she had had her tits squeezed by the odd businessman friend of her father's, and he had laughed and shaken his head because it sounded pathetic, and he had no stake in it, but somehow he felt that Rosie should not be having her tits pulled about by anyone. He protested. He wanted to punch someone. He told Sonia in bed that night how shocked he felt and she replied, "Look, it's not really any of your business. She copes very well with things like that, I'd say. Better than you do. She's old enough, she'll be all right." He felt the contradictions churning away in his head. That was what Georgina had always said about Rosie: "She's old enough."

82
STAFFING CUTS

In February the Department announced that it had had to make staffing cuts and Sonia would not be re-employed.

"Well, that's that, then," she said bitterly. "Things have run their course and now I can go to the UK and finish my research." She looked pale and dull.

Feeling panicky, feeling that he hadn't expected this, Robert suggested to her that they should have a holiday at The Point before term started. They could call in to see her mother at the farm. They could hire a boat and take it around to The Point. They would talk things over.

There was a rusted utility with mismatching doors in the yard of the farm when they arrived, and an old farmer with his hat pushed back and his boot soles secured with wire walked off the verandah to greet them. A diminutive woman sat in the utility, staring furiously at something in the distance. "Oh, Christ," said Sonia. "It's Murray. He's our neighbour. A few years ago when our chimney caught alight he helped out, and now he comes over to poke his nose in. He's awful. That poor, pathetic woman."

"Just on my way round the sheep," said the man, leaning in the car window to speak to them. "Everything jake?" His hands left a smear of grease on the door.

"I don't know, Murray," said Sonia. "We've only just arrived."

"Knocked," said Murray, "but your mum must still be in bed. How's my girl," he said, suddenly leaning in and putting his arm around Sonia. "Still as beautiful as ever."

Perhaps he doesn't see me as a boyfriend, thought Robert. Perhaps he thinks I'm some effete relative or other. Perhaps he hasn't noticed me at all. "Amazing," Robert said.

"Got a kiss for your Uncle Murray?" said Murray.

"Grow up, Murray," said Sonia. "Stop being an old perve."

Murray started saying that they had better come with him to see a fence that needed mending. "Or you'll have all my bloody sheep around the house. Hop in," he said, picking up his sheep dog that was shivering under the utility, its tail flat against its belly like a growth. "Bloody red whore of a useless cunt of a fucking dog," he said, punching the dog's head and hoisting it into the back with a thud.

"Stop it, Murray," said Sonia.

"Ah, bit of swearing never hurt anyone," he said. "All set?"

Sonia sat on Robert's lap and next to them, like a terrified child, sat Murray's wife. She didn't say a word or react to anything that her husband said. "So, what have you been doing at that university of yours, eh? Been revolting, I bet. Get it?" Between gear changes he leaned across his wife and patted Sonia's leg.

They helped Murray strain up the wires in a weak section of the fence. It was on a rise and Robert could see the sea. The Point was far away on the horizon and was smudged by smoke from a bushfire burning somewhere on the other side of it. He reminded himself to listen to the news that night.

After they fixed the fence, Murray drove them back to the farm where they had to make him a cup of coffee and sit with him on the verandah while he drank it. His wife sat in the utility. "She don't want one," he said, jerking his head.

Golda ran her nose around Murray's utility, across the lawn and over his boots and ankles. He put down his cup and waggled Golda's nose to and fro. Golda gave a tiny surprised yelp, backed away, snuffled and shook her way up to him again. Murray flicked her face with her tail and blinded her with her own ears. "That's enough, Murray," said Miriam, leaning out of the kitchen window. Golda wagged her foolish tail.

Then Murray pulled the dog's tail to lift her rear off the ground, gave sharp claps to each side of her head, tipped her over and lifted her up by her paws, two in each hand, and threw her into the horse trough.

"Jesus, Murray," said Robert.

"Golda!" said Sonia.

She struck Murray, kicking and punching him before he could get away from her.

"Christ, Sonia," he said, aggrieved, "that bloody hurt."

Murray tipped out his coffee and accelerated away in his utility. His sheep dog rocked in the back, looking at them, forlorn and embarrassed.

Robert squatted down with Miriam and Sonia to fuss over Golda, who was obsequious on her back. "Well, you were a great help," said Sonia.

83

Aspect had Changed

There was a strong smell of bushfire in the air when they got to The Point, but Robert was certain that the hot wind would continue to blow away from them. It seemed to be dying down, he said, as he looked over the cliff at their hired boat bobbing in the little cove beneath them.

At midnight they decided that the smoke was getting thicker. They could hear the fire coming and Sonia cried out that she could see glowing twigs streaming before the wind. They went outside to look. "Trees are *banging*," she said. "Oh fuck." In the reddish darkness Robert thought she looked diminished, as though she found herself under the scrutiny of a relentless eye. "Come on, Rob. Let's get away."

They heard a neighbour's house ignite, and then Robert's windows and roof seemed to explode. Things hit his head. A terrible wind rushed through, pinching, searing his lungs and eyes. They left everything and Sonia tumbled Robert down the path to the beach, hauled the aluminium dinghy into the water and pushed off. Embers steamed in the sea and settled on their skins.

They climbed onto the boat. Robert, head throbbing, was shocked by the noise and redness he could see on the black cliff top. He sat wordless on the deck. But within two hours he couldn't stop talking: "Are you all right? Fuck the house. I don't want to think about it. Let's just sail off somewhere in the morning." Sonia bathed his scalp. Until late into the night he talked about the fire, blaming himself, the shire council, the house's designers, fate, and himself again, until Sonia told him to shut up.

They bobbed in the boat through the red night and woke with a lively feeling in the morning. The cliffs looked lower, their aspect had changed. Sonia mopped the ashy scum off the deck and asked, "Don't you think we should go up and look at the house?" "No," he told her. "Let's just sail off. We've got everything we need." She looked troubled and shook her head as she made the boat ready to sail.

A sense of loss was nudging at him and memories were threatening to emerge. He didn't feel like being sensible. He didn't want Sonia to be worried on his account. "I'm all right," he said.

They sailed the day away, stopping for lunch and dinner in little fishing ports. Sonia was solicitous, surprising Robert with grave kisses and touching her tongue to the salt spray on his neck. She warned him about sunburn and rubbed oil into his back, and while he sat on the deck she sturdily put the boat to rights or pricked his nostrils with ground-coffee smells from the galley. Robert badly wanted to continue with the holiday: there was the ocean, the deck salty and varnished, white paint slapped thickly on all the surfaces, their rush through the water. He felt expansive and told her that he loved her. "That's enough," she said.

He took stock of her often. In harbours she wore a bikini but when they were far out she tossed it like scraps into a coiled hawser. He watched her dive into the sea with a kind of plump grace after they had made love on the deck. Little tumescences bothered Robert during the day: he half wanted her to see them, but not now when she had a lot to do. A silly pair of running shoes on her feet, she stooped and lashed things together. In the licking breeze of their passage upon the open sea, she unconsciously touched herself. Robert pulled up his leg so that she would not see.

The day passed. In each of the two fishing towns they visited, Robert saw a little man with no neck walking on the jetty with two severe, dismal women with no necks. They did not talk or look at one another. Robert joked with Sonia about things in threes haunting him, and she grimaced after he had said it too often — she was too busy, she said.

His moods ceased their wild swings. He sat on the deck, letting the sun warm him. The day passed and he began to dream and store up memories of what he had lost. When Sonia called out to him to help her manoeuvre the boat, he didn't hear her.

"Robert," she said. "Snap out of it. Look, I think we should go back. This is stupid."

"Tomorrow," he said. "Or the day after."

They moored in a fishing town for the night. Very early the next morning a fishing boat came in and woke them up and told them to moor somewhere else. They had forgotten to buy milk and Robert stared at the empty milk carton in his hands, unable to shake off his mood. Sonia was strained. "This is bloody stupid, Robert," she said. "I'm taking you back to the house." She switched off the transistor radio and asked him if he did not think one news service was enough, the fire was out, stop fiddling with the dial. "Do you want a hand?" he asked, too passive to lift or fold or wind things. She shook her head. She was disappointed in him.

Silently she sailed them back to The Point. The dying fall of Robert's memories paralysed him and he sat in the sun with his back against the cabin, knowing that he should be helping Sonia with the lines and boom. He had a sudden image of himself as a foolish older man, too old for Sonia, and of the string of small disappointments he was making her endure.

84
THE ONES WHO KNOW

Two days before Sonia was due to catch her plane she rang Robert to invite him to a farewell dinner that night at her mother's house in the city. When he arrived Sonia kissed him and then ushered him into the living-room to meet her grandmother Runya, some aunts, friends, and three elderly uncles who sat in a corner and smiled as the dark, handsome women flashed and laughed. They all lavished their love on Sonia and, as Robert stood by diffidently, they reached out to draw him into their circles, not quite catching everything that he said.

He felt a little dowdy up close to them: expressive hands drew him away from his shy positions by the door or on the far side of the piano, affectionate, clever faces looked up into his face and interrupted him, and a newcomer asked him to hold a clasp-bag that was so soft the leather seemed to run between his fingers.

After dinner the old men left to go somewhere. Runya and three other old women sat with relief around a card table, discussing their game but also directing loud, loving remarks to Sonia and talking about a television documentary they wished to watch. Sonia turned the set on for them. Robert sat in an armchair, Sonia and Miriam on the floor against his legs, sharing an ashtray and talking quietly together. The older women called Robert the resident expert, "professor", and asked him questions about the documentary — but he soon realised that he had to go carefully for they had a stake in the film's story, and he found himself being corrected or contradicted or gently chastised: "Books, they tell you nothing," the old women said. "They should listen to the ones who know." They had no time for the names, dates and theories that Robert listed and there was nothing that he could tell them about the horror being depicted, because how could he even *begin* to know — his sympathy was tame, apologetic stuff — and Robert felt that an Aryan ancestor, a Westphalian artisan generations back, had stamped him unmistakably tonight and the old women had seen it, and there was plenty that they could tell him but they did not want to: calm faces, talking clearly on the television screen, were doing that for them.

Robert watched the old women playing cards and saw their eyes slide to the television screen and unwillingly away again as they dealt, shuffled and played their cards.

Runya said suddenly, "I was there."

Robert turned back to the television set and saw children pressing against a wire fence, their fingers patiently hooked to it. The film cut to naked women stooped and running between lines of grainy soldiers, and then cut back to the children again. Their heads were shaven. An officer appeared; he ushered them into lines.

Runya yelled out and her cards dropped around her.

"That was me." She jerked in her chair. "I remember the cameras," she sobbed. "I remember the cameras there." She pointed at herself. "My mother and my sister, they were taken away, and I was for another day kept."

Miriam switched off the television set and consoled Runya. Runya had stopped speaking English, and Miriam, Sonia and the other women crooned to her and replied to her in Yiddish, their voices getting quieter and quieter, circling her with comfort. Half out of his armchair in front of the television set in the far side of the room, Robert did not know what he should do or say. He sat back. After a while he caught Sonia's eye and gave a pantomime of gestures to say that he would go home. At the front door Sonia raised her unhappy face to kiss him goodbye, saying that she had better go back inside and she would see him at the airport.

85
GOING AWAY

Everyone he loved was going away. A few weeks later, flushed with pleasure, Maggie invited him to the pub, where she told him that Brian had been given a London posting for a year and that she had negotiated a year's leave without pay to go with him.

"I'll miss you," said Robert. They had kept an eye on one another, cautioned against foolishness and offered comfort when things went wrong. They confided in each other about love, their spouses and the Department. Robert thought that their tipsy talks in the pub, the hello, goodbye kisses they exchanged even under the cloud of some petty weakness just revealed or some squabble about something, were some of the things that had kept him going.

"I'm selling my car," said Maggie. "Do you want to buy it?"

Robert played with the stem of his glass and thought about it. There was Leigh's twenty-first birthday coming up and a little second-hand car was on his list of possible presents. "All right," he said.

Maggie was getting very tipsy and she waved an unlighted cigarette about.

"It goes really well," she said.

"Sounds fine to me," said Robert.

"And there's nothing wrong with it. Brian always took it in for its service at the proper time, and I've got the receipts for when the brakes were fixed."

Robert leaned forward. "I'm going to buy it, I said."

Maggie concentrated drunkenly on pouring wine into their glasses from the carafe. "But whoever buys it will have to renew the registration soon, I think."

Robert shouted, "Maggie, shut up. I'll buy the bloody thing, all right?"

Maggie's smile filled the room. "Oh, you're going to buy my car. Oh." She lifted her glass to him in a toast.

86
EMBRACE LIFE

On Friday they went to the Edinburgh Castle for a last drink, but Maggie was worried by all the last-minute things she had to do and soon gathered up her bag and cigarettes. "I've got to have sherry with the Dean," she said, waving to the table. "I'll be in on Monday to pick up some books. Bye all."

Robert sat back in his chair, watching students and a sprinkling of his colleagues pouring into the pub, Monica Pabst and Gower among them. He did not want to see either of them. Gower did not seem to know or understand about Georgina or Sonia, and his assumptions and envy were tiresome and inappropriate. Monica Pabst was always asking for extensions of time for her essays but did not ever appear to write anything. Perhaps she thought that an involved discussion in his office about her essay topics would impress itself upon his mind as an actual essay done. But her ideas were loopy, she was in love with life and learning, and she called him "Mr Saxby", which made Robert feel uncomfortable. And yet "Robert" on her lips would sound even worse.

She caught his eye and came across to his table. "Is this seat taken?" she said, sitting down in Maggie's empty chair. "It's really quite amazing how crowded this place gets. Well, you'll be pleased to know, Mr Saxby," she announced, "I'm not going to hit you with anything intellectual today." She slapped her palms on her thighs, as though to state that she was putting her mind behind her and was ready to embrace life itself. She leaned closer and said happily, "Now, you were told to behave yourself yesterday, but I might not be able to manage the same willpower."

Oh, shit, thought Robert. He had made a silly grab at a student yesterday and she had said evenly, "Behave yourself." It was time he stopped doing things like that. Time to tell the Department to go hang. Do something worthwhile, something for himself. He felt so sluggish these days.

Robert went to the bar to buy a jug of beer for his table. He had been afraid to ask what drink Monica Pabst would like to have, but she had wanted beer too. Gower was at the bar looking lost. Robert said, "Look, I have to go now, but there's a group of us sitting over there in the corner. Would you mind taking this jug over for me?" The unexpected always made Gower stop and think. "And I might be speaking out of turn," said Robert, "but Monica Pabst was just talking about you. She's heard about your special subject and wants to do it next year. She wants to meet you, I gather. That's her there, on the left, the blonde one. But she's very shy: don't say I said anything."

Gower's eye gleamed. Robert called out "Thanks" to his departing back.

In the car park he screwed up a leaflet advertising a disco. He asked himself why he should have to go on removing leaflets that people put under his windscreen wipers, or listening to Dick the commissionaire at lunchtime, or eating his mean little breakfasts accompanied by the newspaper and the current-affairs broadcast. He had an oil scuff on his shoe, five minutes passed before he could get his car started, and another five minutes before there was a break in the traffic on the main road. He lived in a messy city. The university could not expand horizontally and so some fancy landscaping had been done to allow for taller buildings. In his letterbox at home was a council note saying the water would be cut off tomorrow for a few hours, but when he tried to fill the kettle he discovered that it was already off.

87

Faceless

He thought that everyone in his profession seemed a little mad these days, and there could be no reason for him to stay in it. He had begun going to the pub at the end of every day and sometimes at lunchtime as well, and there were his colleagues, shell-shocked with strain, hungry to go to bed with the students or mock them bleakly, everyone weary and aggrieved. Everyone desperate to escape and become someone else. The madness was catching, too. Mrs Saxby rang him recently to say that Theresa, her boarder, had been transferred for getting her grade fives to paint the trees in the park pink.

If he didn't do something soon, people would start asking questions. He felt sure the Department must have noticed that he had developed a kind of fragmentary and intermittent interest in things, as though he were only half aware of people, caught only half of what they said to him. The names of his colleagues and students fled from his mind all the time. Monica Pabst had come into his office the day before to ask about footnoting and, as she talked, her face had seemed to dissolve. When he drove home in the afternoons he could scarcely remember the road rules and the streets seemed unfamiliar. From one day to the next, hoardings were erected around holes in the ground, and lately he had been feeling a sensation of whiteness, like snow obscuring his vision.

There could be no point in staying in his job. It was time he took a risk. He could take in some students at an hourly rate when the need arose and never wake up anxious about classes again. He could join a theatre company and might develop a flair for writing short plays, producing them and acting in them, and perhaps sell one or two to radio and television producers. It looked like he would have to sell Degraves Street soon and give Georgina her share, but that was all right — he could buy a small, cheap house or unit and live more economically.

There had been too many days since he failed Ivan, met Georgina, entered his present profession. Those days were often recalled to him because people were talking about Ivan and his Company, his converted-warehouse theatre, his twenty-year struggle with moral guardians, baffled patrons, blinkered reviewers, landlords, bank managers. Robert had seen only two of Ivan's plays. On each occasion Nadine had been selling the tickets; her smile of recognition was a special one flashed down the years. On each occasion Robert had sat, faceless, deep in the back stalls. The first time had been with Georgina, several years ago, and Georgina had been intent on observing the other women walking to their seats. The second time had been a few months ago, with Sonia. She had leaned forward on her seat, absently patting his wrist. On each occasion he had heard the steady breathing next to him, sensed the absorption with the other theatre-goers and the concentration when Ivan stepped from the wings onto the stage or declaimed from the aisle to involve the audience; and on both occasions Robert had recalled Ivan twenty-five years ago, that abject time, his own cravenness.

88
Nice Lines

Georgina seemed to have something on her mind the day she unexpectedly arrived in her red car to visit Robert at The Point. He was alone that weekend, trying to be useful with a paint brush and loading up a trailer with bits and pieces that the builders had left behind.

"Just called to say hello," she said, "and see what progress you've been able to make with the rebuilding. It's almost finished, isn't it? It looks lovely. It's a nice design."

Robert made her a drink, asking himself if she was

following up that ambiguous dinner and whether or not he cared; he decided that he did but he suppressed the thought and told himself to be realistic. She did not have that speculative look in her eye, and besides, before they went on their walk she just happened to ask if he had had the phone reconnected because she had to ring to say she would be late. And when she made the call she cloaked the receiver with her hand and said something into it in a chuckling murmur about be sure to save me some lobster, I'll be back in time for dinner.

But, apart from that, they had a pleasant time reminiscing, walking to the shop and back again by way of the beach, tut-tutting about the scorched pine trees and devastated town, swapping stories about the kids (she told him they would be sending him an invitation to Leigh's birthday party soon — Mr Saxby was going to print them, she said). Later they sat in the bamboo lounge chairs in the enormous sunroom that smelled of new pine boards that were still heaped with sawdust. Through one glass wall Robert could see the sea and through the other the red Mercedes sports car that Alan had given Georgina.

She caught his look, smiled and asked him if Mrs Saxby was pleased about the election result last month. She chuckled at a memory: "I drove the Mercedes straight up to the polling booth, parked right out the front, and you should have seen the look on the Liberal fellow's face when I walked right past him and took a how-to-vote card from the Labor fellow." She gave a light laugh. "It felt really good." She looked at the car from her chair by the window. "It's got nice lines, hasn't it?"

All this was by way of introducing what she had come down to say to him: "I suppose you could tell when we had dinner that time that I was pretty unhappy, couldn't make up my mind about things, etcetera, etcetera. You know. Anyhow, it's been settled now — Alan and I are getting married next month. I sort of needed to see you that day to work something out."

Well, wacky doo. But could she be more specific? Ha.

Probably someone — Alan — had once expressed to her some bullshit philosophy about never apologise, never explain, and, being a natural coward, she had adopted it too. Fucking bad news, these little chats with Georgina at the beach in winter. She always seemed to come up with something flattening.

89
SECOND LOOKING

Robert likes to walk a set route for exercise when he gets tired of rattling around inside Degraves Street. His aim is to walk on grass as much as possible. He will cross the front lawn, leap onto the nature strip and then turn left, walking down the hill to the park where he can indulge himself. If he sees joggers he walks with his head down so that they will have to swerve to avoid him.

He is building up to making a decision about the Department, and soon he will sell the house in Degraves Street and buy a small house close to the centre of the city. There will not be many more walks like this.

In the park he likes to stand and take a last look. The sun in the early mornings burns away the mist as though it were lifting the lid on this dirty old town, revealing the sodden tissues, a thong and scraps of cellophane. He thinks that he lives in a mean landscape and it had got worse as his children grew up. Small children are expected to play on odd, bobbing heads on stiff, black springs, or in plastic forts. There are grinning faces painted on fences, and pine and bark chips scattered around. The park has been scraped smooth, stripped of anything tangled or haphazard, so that fathers on fortnightly access to their children run less risk of needing to dab a wet corner of their handkerchiefs at a grazed knee. Eight years ago a freeway on legs appeared across the bottom corner of the park. Robert is tired of seeing the aged hippie slowly uncoil and breaststroke the air as though he is picking himself out of a vat of molasses. What the man is doing is called tai chi, but Robert does his best to prevent the words entering his head.

He walks under the freeway, touching his hand to a concrete pillar supporting it, feeling the traffic rumbling overhead. The whole city is decaying. One morning there was a pink sweat-band on the ground. Robert wished torn muscles on its owner.

He leaves the park. He looks in the windows as he passes through the shopping centre. The only shop open early on Sunday mornings is the milk bar. The shopping centre is probably dying. In Robert's street, for example, the elderly people and misfits like himself stay on, but most people do not live there for very long. There do not seem to be many children these days, apart from Nat, the serious little boy from next door, whose voice is a deep growl and whose parents will not allow a television set inside their house. They tell Robert this. Recently, on a Sunday morning, Robert had awoken to the sounds of a fatuous song and maniacal voices. He stumbled into his lounge-room to find Nat, slack-jawed in pyjamas, in front of the television set, watching the Sunday-morning clown show. They have come to an arrangement.

This morning Nat raced through Robert's house to the backyard, yelling for his pet rabbit. But Robert had already seen the squashed body on the road outside and made a mental note to ring the council to send someone to collect the body. They are funny people next door. Robert asked them if they would be burying the body of their pet and they said no. Perhaps it was because a few cars had done their work during the night and welded the fur to the tar.

Thinking these things Robert passes the second-hand furniture shop and sees a print of the painting of the Eurasian woman with the green face, and he hurries past. He wonders who comes to buy things at the antiquarian bookseller's or the manchester shop. There is some vomit on the footpath from last night, and an empty bottle in a brown paper bag. A man hoses down the cars in the used-car lot and another vacuums them. Do they do that every day? Robert thinks about the people who come to the car yard on Sunday mornings, holding yesterday's *Saturday Car Mart* with its advertisements circled in ball-point pen, devoting Sunday to the used-car yards because they have established that all the privately advertised cars are lemons. Robert has been looking at small cars lately and wondering if he has done the right thing in buying Maggie's little car to give to Leigh for his twenty-first birthday.

Robert is walking under the railway overpass when an empty train rackets along above him, slowing for the station. The din is stupefying; he hunches away from it, his shoulder brushing against some graffiti that doesn't appear to make sense. The electrical-appliance shop has clock radios in the window. When he first met Sonia he had watched time drag on her bedside clock: but now that he thinks about it, Sonia's electric clock was of an older kind, with white numbers painted on little black flags that constantly changed, indicating each new hour and minute with a tiny, friendly, flip sound.

And so it is that Robert automatically looks into the sunless alley that runs between the electrical-appliance shop and the aquarium shop. There is no need to look twice. The shoes and ankles are plain enough, the hands are hidden beneath the body, and there is enough blood thickening under the head for Robert to smell a violence perpetrated there last night next to the empty pop-up toaster cartons.

90

PROBABLY

Robert calls in to show Mr and Mrs Saxby the little car he is giving Leigh. They admire it, give him a cup of tea and tell him they will see him at the party Georgina and Alan are giving Leigh.

Robert hedges. "I'll probably see you there," he says. "I'll try to drop in for a short time."

Mrs Saxby smiles, understanding him. Mr Saxby says, "Did you get the invitation, son? Nice job, wasn't it, one of the nicest I've ever printed."

They talk about Georgina for a while. "She dropped in the other day," says Mrs Saxby. "She's less stand-offish now that she's got someone else's money to spend."

Robert utters a faint, shocked snigger.

91

DIRTY OLD TOWN

It is Leigh's birthday and Robert and Rosie are taking him to lunch. Robert is the first to arrive at the restaurant. While he waits he wonders if there is something one should say to one's son on his twenty-first birthday, some advice or joke or intimacy that will let them become friends, something more he can offer apart from handing over the keys to a little car.

Rosie arrives and they kiss. He is pleased that they see each other regularly, but he is perplexed by matters of time and the stages at which one achieves certain things, and was he or wasn't he ever ambitious enough, for his daughter seems poised beyond her years, is teaching a senior class, and buying a house. He can't understand how this can be but it is true, she is. And the thought of his daughter in her own house, and his daughter with her own children growing up and having children who will not want to sit next to their ancient relative at the dinner table, leaves Robert feeling that he is existing on a different plane in time. After all, his face in the mirror doesn't seem to change.

They are chatting when Leigh bursts into the restaurant, bringing with him sodden scraps of leaves and paper clinging to his shoes. A smell of bus fumes rises from his coat. A waiter says, "Allow me, sir," and bears the coat away.

"Dirty old town," says Robert. He stands up and Leigh shakes hands warily and leans forward for Rosie's kiss. They chorus, "Happy birthday!" and Robert says, "Here," handing his son the car keys and explaining. It has been his big secret and he enjoys seeing Leigh's overwhelmed face.

Robert orders three bottles of champagne and slowly he begins to feel disburdened for the first time in weeks. His children look full of life and seem to appreciate him, the food is good, no-one has to be anywhere for a few hours and the champagne is just the thing.

During dessert Leigh's girlfriend materialises. She sits close to Leigh, holding onto his arm, her face following everything that he says or does. She is rather silly and wispy. Robert wishes Sonia were here. It is time he stopped drinking. He empties the last bottle of champagne into the glasses of the young ones. Waiters are gathering in a disapproving line by the door to the kitchen. It is half-past three.

Leigh starts to mumble something, an apology and explanation about tonight: "The party Mum and Alan are giving me is pretty big really; there will be security guards keeping an eye on everything," and "Do you know how to get there?" Robert says he is sure he can find it. He cannot tell Leigh that he has driven past his mother's new house now and then, has parked nearby from time to time recently. "It would be nice if you brought someone with you, Dad. Are you still seeing Sonia? Would she like to come?"

92

INNER EYE

I suppose I could go, thinks Robert. He thinks of others at the party who might catch at his presence and lean just that little bit towards his corner. He has days like that, when he strides across the world and it stops in his wake. There are days when he is slicked clean with water, his body like a dancer's, and he thinks of sitting with someone at a little corner table, showing her half of his calm face in the candlelight; but he meets no-one and no-one is there to share his beauty with him when he leaves the house.

He goes into his bedroom and selects a white shirt and a deep blue tie from his wardrobe. He tries them on with his beautiful suit. He stands in front of his mirror to gauge the effect, but his inner eye is too cluttered, he feels washed with a sensation of coldness and white snow, and he cannot judge.

93
WIDDERSHINS ABOUT

Robert Saxby is cold, sitting in his parked car under a plane tree on this July night. At intervals there are street lights — one is flickering on and off perversely and it is best not to look at it — and dark houses which do not announce themselves, even in daylight, because of their brick walls and high hedges. Any gleam on Robert's car has been dulled by the accumulating dampness. There is a security man blowing whitely onto his cold fingers outside the crested gates to the driveway of the house on which Robert is spying. In one hand the man holds a torch that he will use to examine party invitations such as the crumpled one stuffed in Robert's glove-box. It is not yet half-past seven. Robert and the security man are the only people in the street. Otherwise there is nobody and nothing but the shadows and patches of roadway artificially lit, ready to accommodate the cars of many party guests. Robert looks at his watch again. There is plenty of time yet before the first guests begin to arrive: time enough to change his mind, dig the invitation out of the glove-box and smooth out its wrinkles over his knee. Drinks at half-past seven, it says, beautifully printed by Mr Saxby, dinner and dancing from eight o'clock, Georgina's new address in italics at the bottom.

Robert winds down his window a little and hears householders calling their pets to be fed or tied up. A child walking a dog in the cold evening air walks past Robert sitting in his car and looks curiously at him. Perhaps the child wonders why there is a man sitting in a car and perhaps he knows that Robert's car does not usually park in this street.

Robert does not belong here, and he thinks about the places where he can belong. He will tell the Department to go hang, sell the house in Degraves Street, become an actor. He has had enough of standing uncertainly in the wings. He would like to be able to say, at the end, that he seized the moment, changed course before regret had set in. Waiting for things to change, waiting on the brink of a major shift in things, he wonders if all the little things will change too: no more going to bed so early; better meals; visits to friends; clothes he feels comfortable in; no more silly thoughts.

An idea: he will join a theatre company and ask the members to stay with him at the beach house so that they can all rehearse together. He will not be a flouncy actor nor a fawning one, or be dilletantish or egotistical — he will just be a serious professional. He will not let someone good for him slip away again. And what a stage the area around The Point will make: the burnt trees developing a fluff of new shoots on their branches, the pine trees with their scorched skirts, the destroyed town with here and there a black chimney persisting in the ashes.

And perhaps having friendly people in the beach house might serve to settle the turbulent spirits that seem to be agitating in all the rooms there lately. One friendly ghost keeps turning off his reading light, giving him darkness when he wants light, but once lighting the bay window when he came in the door, as if in welcome. Sure, the switch is faulty, but Robert knows enough about electricity to have done a good job when he fixed it last week. Perhaps the spirits share his distress at the loss of familiar things. A few days after the fire he had found the gold letter-opener that Georgina had given him lying undamaged in the ashes, and he had been reminded of all the things he would never get back.

Robert does not like to think that he might get tiresome and useless enough for the young ones to want him to die as the best thing all round. And certainly he does not want anyone to find him in some alley with his head bashed in: just fancy the ignominy of being found by some inoffensive, forgettable passer-by, his wits perhaps dulled by brooding on his own unloved, lonely state, whose uttered sob is more for himself than it is for you; and a newspaper item somewhere at the bottom of page six reporting you as an unidentified man and listing the clothes you were wearing; probably one of these young punks done it, said a shopkeeper, and no clues amongst the empty cartons in the alley; and the police cannot justify spending too much time on it; and when no-one comes forward to claim your body or identify it you are shoved into a pauper's grave, paid for by the city.

Suddenly Robert sinks lower in his car. He has seen a car he recognises as Georgina's leave the driveway of the house with the crested gates. The security guard waves; probably someone has had to go on a last-minute errand. Maybe they forgot to buy ice. Robert giggles.

It is pretty silly of him to be sitting here parked at the top of the street in a shadow between street lights, but he tells himself it is a once-only lapse. Really, everything is happenstance. He has taken to making the response: "I'll believe it when I see it," to the things that people say to him: Sonia, just about to board a plane and get on with her life, clasping his head in her hands to say, "It was good; I'm glad. I'll keep in touch; and things will get better for you, you'll see"; the insurance assessors looking at the ashy remains of the beach house; the awful Monica Pabst in his office, tearing her hair out over a late essay; his father thinking he will print and publish books at last instead of wedding invitations; Georgina listening to him consideringly and saying, "Point taken, point taken."

He fills in time. In his head Georgina nods in remorse as he ticks off the charges. He wants to give her the imagination to really look at herself for the first time. He wants to see her face register realisation and shame. But it is too cold in the car, the darkness seems like snow cutting out the light and he loses concentration. Robert has told himself he will wait, watch the first guests arrive for the party and then steal away home, nothing more.

He expects that Georgina will send him photographs of Leigh for the family album. He hopes that they will not be too posed. Robert likes best candid photographs of people going about their everyday lives because he knows that, once they are in a photograph, they are isolated: from the smells clinging to the clothes of someone walking by, the sound of a door closing just to the left of them, the discreet tug to ease a brassiere strap in another room, someone's satisfaction with her lot.

Robert likes to develop his own photographs, likes to see images swirl into existence in his darkroom sink. Sometimes he is unfaithful to the camera, taking an image and turning it widdershins about, or his red hands in the red hush of his darkroom perform interferences, tricks and accidents. Sometimes his ghost sits on his shoulder, impulsive and tinkering, causing a kink in things.

When he walks down streets now, they teem with an everyday mess of sly pimps' eyes, stickybeaks, the bottleman with his pet magpie on his shoulder, a dog stretching first her front legs and then her hind legs, a businessman's skinny ankles, boredom and lust on all the faces, the murdered man's head caked to a blood pool and his hands tucked sleep-fashion under his thighs, face down at dawn in that alley running alongside the electrical-appliance shop. The streets make these confidences to Robert and he walks along the beach later working out how he can pass them on, thinking that there is something extraordinary and uncomfortable about everything.

He watches the first cars stopping and driving away again outside Alan's house. There probably is a lot of room in the house for a party, and there will be no gate-crashers because the man in uniform at the gate is not letting cars in and is checking invitations of guests after they have parked their cars in the street and walked back to him. He lets them pass and they walk to the hidden house up a curving driveway glistening because it is raining gently. Robert recognises some of the guests. They stamp their feet and blow on their cold hands while their invitations are checked; some older guests are in dinner suits and cocktail dresses with warm wraps around their shoulders, and the young ones are gaunt and insubstantial under the street lights, almost ill-looking. But their hair and clothes are bright and celebratory, they have presents for Leigh wrapped in thick paper and Robert supposes that they will get some colour into their skins when they get inside with the lights and music. He wonders how long the security man is expected to stand there in the cold and the wet.